"I think we might be trapped in here," Jacob said

Instead of being upset at the idea, Amanda felt a warm thrill go through her. She *so* wasn't thinking straight.

He was breathing faster now as his gaze traveled the length of her. "I need to warn you that I'm not feeling in control of myself here." He stalked over toward her and she braced herself, expecting him to kiss her, hoping he'd kiss her. Instead, he breezed past her to a small table where there was a heavy brass candleholder. Holding it out to her, he said, "Preventative measures."

"For what?" she asked, taking the candlestick.

"You need to knock me out. Bash me on the head. Then you'll be safe. I don't want to do anything I'm going to regret."

At her puzzled look, he continued. "I don't want to force myself on you. I feel an overwhelming compulsion to throw you on the bed over there and take you hard and fast. It's close to uncontrollable. So knock me out while you have the chance."

She considered the candlestick for a moment, then slowly put it down. Then, holding his gaze, she took his hand and guided it to her breast....

Blaze™

Dear Reader,

Hot Spell, my first book for Harlequin Blaze, was inspired by three little words spoken on a talk show about how love can "feel like magic."

Jacob Caine and Amanda LaGrange are clearly—at least to me and their matchmaking boss—meant for each other. But because of that stubborn streak both of them have, self-protection, denial, practicality, the wrong thing said at the wrong time—or *all of the above*—they're going to need a little push.

A little...*magical*...push.

Thanks to an enchanted grandfather clock the two paranormal investigators uncover in a haunted house at the stroke of midnight, they're going to find out exactly how much love can feel like magic—whether they're ready for that particular discovery or not.

I'm thrilled to not only get the chance to write for my favorite Harlequin line, but to have my release during their sixtieth anniversary celebrations. It's truly an honor!

Happy reading...

Michelle Rowen

Michelle Rowen

HOT SPELL

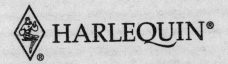

TORONTO • NEW YORK • LONDON
AMSTERDAM • PARIS • SYDNEY • HAMBURG
STOCKHOLM • ATHENS • TOKYO • MILAN • MADRID
PRAGUE • WARSAW • BUDAPEST • AUCKLAND

PLEASE RECYCLE · THIS PRODUCT IS RECYCLABLE

Recycling programs
for this product may
not exist in your area.

ISBN-13: 978-0-373-79507-9

HOT SPELL

This edition published by arrangement with Harlequin Books S.A.

® and TM are trademarks of the publisher. Trademarks indicated with ® are registered in the United States Patent and Trademark Office, the Canadian Trade Marks Office and in other countries.

www.eHarlequin.com

Printed in U.S.A.

ABOUT THE AUTHOR

Michelle Rowen is an award-winning, bestselling author of multiple paranormal romance novels, including the Immortality Bites vampire series. *Hot Spell* is her first book for Harlequin Blaze. A voracious but picky reader, TV viewer and movie watcher, she prefers all her entertainment to include a happily-ever-after...or else! Michelle is currently in treatment for serious Twitter and Facebook addictions. Please visit her online at www.michellerowen.com.

Thank you to my editor Brenda Chin and fellow Blaze authors Kelley St. John and Alison Kent for all their help and general fabulousness.

_1_

AMANDA LAGRANGE shook her head so vigorously it felt as though it might come loose from her shoulders. "Please, not him. _Anyone_ but him."

"Jacob's the only agent currently available, and we need this house investigated tonight. The owner paid extra for an immediate assessment." Patrick McKay's voice was firm.

It was pointless to argue. Knowing Patrick, her boss, there was no way she'd be able to get out of this. Besides, making a fuss about her last official assignment for the Paranormal Assessment and Recovery Agency would make her look childish.

She finally sighed. "Okay, fine. I'll do it."

"I don't understand why you two can't stand each other after all this time. Why is that again?" Patrick sounded both curious and distracted. He was a born multitasker, and was currently having a conversation with Amanda while he replied to a long list of text messages from other agents on his BlackBerry.

"It's...it's just...many reasons. Too many to list."

PARA had hired Jacob Caine two years ago because of his empathic abilities. He could get a sense of people and places just by touch. Before that, he'd worked as a private detective for five years. Both talents came in very handy at an agency that investigated paranormal phenomena. PARA agents were often called in to assess haunted properties and cursed or enchanted objects, and would then take the necessary precautions to ensure no one was harmed.

Jacob had it easy, like many of the other agents in-house. He hadn't even known he was psychic until recently.

Amanda? Not so much.

She'd seen her first ghost—and had a pleasant conversation with him, in fact—when she was only eight years old. At the time, it had been natural and not scary at all. However, that encounter had led to many others in quick succession, and some of the ghosts weren't as friendly as the first. Her frightened parents had tried to get her to stop, but it wasn't as though she'd been trying to attract otherworldly attention—it just happened. Ghosts were drawn to her. One ghost, annoyed at being interrupted by her father, had pushed him down a flight of stairs. Luckily, other than a twisted ankle, he wasn't injured, but the event did its damage in another way.

Not able to deal with his daughter being a "ghost-magnet freak," which was how he'd put it at the time, Ed LaGrange had packed his bags and left Amanda and her mother that very night. She'd never spoken to him again.

The memory still brought a painful lump of emotion to her throat.

Her mother blamed Amanda and her clairvoyant ability for shattering their home. Amanda grew up feeling like more of an outcast every day of her childhood. Her being different had destroyed her family.

Being at school didn't help, either. Normal kids gave her the nickname "Amanda the Strange," which, while not a terribly original taunt, came to represent verbally everything she hated about herself. She was a freak—she was *strange*.

Therefore, she had tried as hard as possible to ignore her psychic abilities. It had worked for a while, at least until PARA came to her college looking for potential agents. Patrick McKay had seen Amanda's file, met with her personally, and offered her enough money to justify dipping back into her despised abilities.

Other than the money, the bright side of working for PARA was that there were other agents who subsequently became her good friends—kind of like a bizarre extended family. She was invited to their weekly "tequila and séance" parties. She'd gone a couple of times since her best friend Vicky, another clairvoyant, rarely took no for an answer in pushing Amanda to get out and have more fun, but it wasn't really her scene.

Even though she was surrounded by happy psychics who liked her and who she liked in return, she'd never gotten over her father's rejection and her childhood traumas. It had made her the woman she was today, for better or for worse.

As far as her dating life—well, she tried not to tell her boyfriends about her psychic abilities at first—or at all, if possible. PARA agents were a close-knit group, but "normal men" outside that circle didn't understand or were scared off by anything unusual—just like her father and schoolmates had been. When Amanda's boyfriends found out her secret, they usually found the nearest exit as quickly as possible.

And then there was Jacob Caine. Decidedly *not* a normal man.

She'd met him at a staff party held at O'Grady's, a local pub, two years ago, shortly after he'd moved to the area and joined the agency. Her friends, especially Vicky, had already told her how hot the new recruit was, how devastatingly charming, and how most of them—the single or even not so single—wanted to have extremely imaginative sex with him. Like, *immediately*.

And he was. *Hot,* that is. Darkly attractive with short, scruffy black hair and flashing green eyes framed with thick black lashes. He dressed casually—no tie for him. She could vividly recall his navy-blue shirt being unbuttoned at the neck that night to reveal a glimpse of his obviously chiseled torso. He was six feet tall with broad shoulders, lean hips...and an *amazing* ass.

At least, that had been her first impression.

Instant attraction.

Amanda's mouth had literally watered at the sight of him despite the fact she wasn't usually romantically drawn to fellow psychics. Then again, she'd been celibate for over a year after a bad break-up—another guy who'd freaked at the thought she could talk to ghosts—so she was certain that was to blame for her heightened sensitivity to such a fine specimen of male hotness.

From across the room, Jacob caught her staring and their eyes met. She was sure he'd be able to tell just from a glance that she wanted to climb onto his gorgeous body and do things to him she wouldn't even trust to her diary.

He disengaged from the throng of cleavage-revealing women and came toward her with his hand extended.

"I'm Jacob," he said without losing her gaze. "And you are?"

"Amanda." She inhaled sharply as she felt the strength and warmth of his long fingers wrap around hers. An unbidden surge of desire curled inside her. His aftershave was a spicy musk with just a hint of cinnamon and a whole lot of man.

He frowned, but she had no idea why. Maybe it was because she was practically drooling on him.

Pull yourself together, she commanded herself.

"Something wrong?" she asked when his grip tightened.

"No..." But his frown deepened as he looked down at her hand. "It's odd. It's like you have a psychic wall up around yourself. I normally get a sense of someone when I touch them for the first time, but I'm getting nothing from you at all."

"You can get something from me if you come over here!" Vicky called from their far left before laughing suggestively. Amanda repressed a smile and an eye-roll at her friend's enthusiasm and returned her attention to the gorgeous man in front of her.

"No walls, I assure you," she said. "Maybe I'm just special."

His eyes snapped back up to hers. "Maybe you are." The frown disappeared, replaced instead by a killer smile. "Amanda, you said?"

"That's right."

He nodded. "They already told me about you. You're the one they call Amanda the Strange, right?"

She tensed. "It's LaGrange. But yeah, that's me. Strangeness incorporated."

An ice-cold sensation immediately swept over her at the sound of the despised nickname that represented everything about her that she hated. Why would he say that to her? To get some sort of a reaction? And who'd told him that?

So much for letting down her guard and getting drunk on tequila with Vicky and the gang last week and sharing soul-crushing childhood stories. That wouldn't happen again.

She finally yanked her hand back from Jacob's. He looked at her oddly.

"Is there something wrong?" he asked.

"Wrong?" Her jaw felt tight. "No, of course not. I...uh, I have to go."

Damn, she'd been having such a good night, too. How was it possible that three little words could ruin everything?

Jacob grabbed her wrist. "I thought we might be able to talk for a bit."

So he could insult her more? Yeah. That sounded like a plan.

"I guess you thought wrong," she said, the iciness in her voice matching the chill she felt inside. "There are lots of women here who will be happy to talk to you. Or *more,* if you like. Trust me, you won't miss me."

"Amanda, wait—"

She fixed a frozen smile on her face. She needed to get out of there. "Welcome to PARA, Jacob. I'm sure everyone will be as delighted to meet you as I've been."

He raised a dark eyebrow. "Is that sarcasm I hear?"

"You're very insightful. You must be psychic."

He studied her closely. "I guess first impressions are misleading. I thought we might hit it off."

Amanda had no idea why she wanted to cry. Why was she letting this guy affect her so strongly? It felt as though he could see right through to the vast and varied weaknesses she tried desperately to hide from everyone. Hell, maybe she did put up psychic walls around herself without even realizing it.

Just being near him suddenly made her very uncomfortable.

She gave him a practiced withering look that helped to hide when she was feeling more than a little vulnerable. "I guess you thought wrong."

"Well, then, it was delightful meeting you, too, Amanda." He turned away, but then glanced back over his shoulder, his green eyes narrowed. "By the way, that was also sarcasm."

And then he returned to his waiting swarm of admirers and didn't look back.

Vicky ran over to see how everything had gone during her conversation with the new hottie. Amanda had kept her answers vague and then excused herself from the party early. She'd had enough.

It was definitely true what they said—don't judge a book by its cover. Jacob Caine had a mighty fine cover, but she wasn't interested in reading any further.

But for a moment there, when their eyes first met...that rare instant attraction she'd felt...

Well, it didn't really matter. Amanda was much too practical to believe in love at first sight.

She'd felt strongly enough about their unpleasant meeting that she'd asked Patrick not to pair her and Jacob for any assignments together and he'd agreed. PARA had over two dozen agents so it was an easy problem to avoid. If she saw Jacob in passing, she'd make polite small talk about the weather or traffic, but even then she tried to get away from him as quickly as possible.

From the tightness in Jacob's jaw whenever they spoke, it was obvious that he wasn't all that fond of her, either.

It was really unfortunate that, despite everything, she still found him as devastatingly attractive as she had the first time she'd seen him.

Annoying, really.

And now, after all this time, Patrick was going to make them work together.

Less than a week and she'd be saying good-bye to her friends at PARA—the ones who made life as a psychic almost bearable—and moving to New York City to work for her boyfriend, David K. Smith, in his advertising agency. Selling advertising was about as far removed from investigating paranormal phenomena as you could get...and that would be a huge relief for her. She was starting her life all over again at the ripe old age of twenty-seven.

While David knew she worked for PARA, he didn't know in what capacity. She hadn't told him she could talk to ghosts at all. Better safe than sorry.

And he didn't have to know. When she left Mystic Ridge for good she'd put her past behind her and get the chance to be completely and totally normal.

Finally.

"Jacob will pick you up outside in ten minutes," Patrick said. He'd finished answering his e-mails while she'd been lost in her thoughts.

He glanced up at her from his high-tech wheelchair. He'd had a run-in with a very unpleasant poltergeist six months ago that had sent him headfirst down a flight of stairs—a scary reminder of what had happened to her father. Patrick was still recovering from a near-fatal spinal cord injury. Since he was a friend, as well as a great boss, Amanda was just happy and relieved he'd lived to tell the tale.

"Are you doing this on purpose?" she asked.

He raised an eyebrow. "What are you talking about?"

"This assignment tonight with Jacob. You're mad I'm leaving, aren't you?"

Patrick put his BlackBerry down on his desk and spread his hands. "You have to do what you have to do, Amanda. As long as you think quitting PARA will make you happy, then I fully support your decision."

She nodded stiffly, swallowing past a huge lump that had formed in her throat. Quitting PARA *would* make her happy—she knew it. The only thing that made it hard was knowing she wouldn't be seeing Patrick, Vicky and the others on a daily basis anymore. "Well, good."

"However, we are throwing you a going-away party." He grinned at her and his blue eyes twinkled with good humor. "And attendance is required. Tuesday night at O'Grady's. Drinks are on me."

She couldn't help but smile at that. Patrick would find any excuse for a party. "I'll be there."

"I'm picking up the cake, too. Got a preference? Chocolate, vanilla...maybe *rum?*"

"Rum," she said as her smile widened. "Definitely rum."

She could use a little bit of the booze right now. It might make spending the rest of her evening with Jacob Caine remotely bearable.

PATRICK WATCHED Amanda leave his office. She was uncomfortable at the prospect of being partnered with Jacob. It was obvious.

But it had to be done.

Maybe it was because he'd been stuck in the damn wheelchair for so long that he'd started interfering in people's lives. Too much time to sit and think...and observe.

Amanda was making a huge mistake by quitting PARA and leaving the friends who loved and accepted her to go off with a man she obviously, to Patrick at least, didn't love.

He saw it in her eyes, a growing dullness, an acceptance that life was not supposed to be extraordinary.

Since his accident, Patrick knew firsthand that life was a gift—every damn day was—and if you didn't accept it, sooner or later it might be snatched away right in front of you.

He'd seen a spark of passion in Amanda's eyes, though. Whenever the beautiful brunette saw Jacob she seemed to fill with life. She claimed to dislike him for reasons she'd never properly explained, but Patrick was far from convinced when that flush came to her cheeks as it had just now. And he'd seen the same intensity in Jacob's gaze, as well.

Patrick rubbed his temples. When exactly had he been appointed resident cupid? Hell if he knew, but it was the least he could do when the evidence presented itself so clearly that the two of them belonged together.

One attempt. That's all they got. Make them work together, make them spend time together before Amanda left for what she considered her shiny new life for good, and see what happened.

Maybe they'd kill each other. That was possible. It might be better than the grudging acceptance both of them seemed to have of their current lackluster lives.

If they were forced to spend a few hours in each other's company, Patrick was fairly certain *something* would happen between them. The only question was...what?

JACOB'S KNUCKLES had already turned white. He gripped the steering wheel of his '68 black Mustang convertible parked at the curb in front of the PARA office and tried to breathe normally.

Even if he had to be stuck with her on this assignment, why exactly had Patrick insisted that they drive to the location together? It was ridiculous. Not to mention stupid. Dumb. Pointless. Annoying. All of the above.

His boss obviously had it in for him to pair him up with Amanda the Strange tonight. Did he want Jacob to quit?

Honestly. If he didn't love his job—the only damn thing in his life that gave him any sense of purpose anymore—then he'd quit in a heartbeat. He didn't need this kind of trouble.

And here she comes now, he thought with a sinking feeling. *Miss Trouble, herself.*

The tall glass doors of the office building opened and Amanda slowly made her way toward his car. He could already feel the ice-blue gaze that seemed to penetrate right down to his very core. Her dark hair was pulled back from her gorgeous face in a sleek ponytail. Long bangs swept over her forehead. Today she wore a thin teal V-neck sweater over blue jeans. *Casual for her,* he thought absently. The sweater was tight enough for him to see clearly the generous swell of her breasts. His own jeans became tighter at the sight of her—but only in the front.

His knuckles whitened even more on the steering wheel.

He hated that she affected him like this. Other than lusting after her body for two years now, he honestly couldn't stand the woman.

Why should he? She obviously despised him.

With one contemptuous look at the party where they first met, Amanda had stared a hole right through him to the other side as if her beautiful baby blues had laser beams hooked up to them. He'd felt naked and exposed, and not in a fun handcuffs-and-bedpost sort of way.

What the hell happened? he wondered, and not for the first time since that night.

He still didn't know. One moment they were introducing themselves to each other and he was falling very quickly into those gorgeous eyes of hers, and the next moment she was giving him the freezing-cold shoulder. He just wished he'd been able to get an empathic read on her. It would have helped to pinpoint exactly what had turned her off about him. She'd said she didn't have psychic walls up to block him, but he was less convinced.

It would make things much easier if he'd been able to forget about her and not want her nearly every day since. What did they say about the unattainable? Made it that much more exciting?

It wasn't exciting. Torturous and uncomfortable, yes. Exciting, no.

She was definitely his weakness. And he had to overcome his pointless attraction to her. Tonight would be a great chance—especially since he'd heard she was quitting PARA soon—to finally get the beautiful clairvoyant out of his system.

Hell, two years ago he hadn't believed in any of this psychic stuff. He'd been a regular guy with a regular job and a fiancée he planned to marry—that is, until he caught her in bed with his best friend. Sounded like the ultimate cliché, but it still stung like hell.

At the time, PARA had been secretly checking out his background. They'd found out he had certain *abilities,* abilities that he'd always written off to intuition and luck, and they offered him a job at exactly the right time. He en- thusiastically took the chance of leaving his old life to come to the small town of Mystic Ridge in upper New York state, where the PARA headquarters were located. But the scars had already formed over his heart. He'd trusted not one but *two* people, and they'd both screwed him over. Or, he supposed, they'd screwed each other and he'd simply been left out in the cold.

Then they'd gotten married four months later claiming that they were madly in love. Insult to injury. Definitely.

His plan for revenge? To drink a great deal of alcohol. Also to have sex with as many women as would let him. To his surprise, there were a whole lot of women who would, which was great for a while, *fantastic* even, at least until he realized that maybe he wanted a bit more than a series of empty one-night stands.

Then he'd met her—Amanda LaGrange—and for the briefest of moments when their eyes met across the room that night he felt his scarred heart start to pound a little faster. At least, until she dug her designer stiletto heel into it.

He took the hint.

Whatever. He was happy working for PARA and having an exciting and varied sex life. It worked for him and he hadn't received any complaints yet.

He tensed as Amanda opened up the passenger-side door of the Mustang and got in. She had a fake, frozen smile plastered on her face. He recognized it. It was the same fake, frozen smile she always wore in his presence.

The smile that made him focus on her full red lips and wonder what they'd taste like.

No, he thought immediately. *She has no effect on you anymore, remember? Be strong.*

"Jacob," she said simply.

"That's my name," he replied. "How've you been, Amanda?"

"Wonderful," she said.

"Good to hear." He shifted into first gear and pulled away from the curb. "I don't think you've ever been in my car before."

"No, I haven't."

And that was about the end of his reserve of small talk. With a two-hour drive ahead of them, that might pose a bit of a problem.

"Patrick briefed me on the assignment earlier and wanted me to fill you in." She reached into the bag she'd brought with her to pull out a notebook filled with page after page of her neat, precise handwriting. "A woman named Sheila Davis recently inherited the property from a distant uncle. While doing a walk-through she heard strange noises and had a sense of being pushed out of the house. That's when she contacted us for an immediate assessment."

"She's scared to live there?"

"No. Actually, she thinks a haunted house will reduce the property value. She wants to sell and turn a quick profit and is planning an open house next week. So we go in, determine if there needs to be an exorcism performed, and then we leave. I figure it won't take more than twenty minutes."

She was wearing that perfume he liked.

Dammit to hell, he thought angrily.

He shifted position in his seat trying to ignore her very warm, feminine presence so close to him. Was it the fact that he knew he couldn't have her that made him feel this way?

But, no. He *didn't* want her. He could have any woman he wanted, and Amanda the Strange was not even on the list anymore.

Vanilla, he thought then. Her perfume smelled like vanilla. Edible. Delicious.

His grip on the steering wheel was so tight by now he thought he might be able to yank it right out of the dashboard if he tried. He realized that taking on this assignment tonight had been a huge, regrettable mistake. But Patrick had practically begged him, and he didn't want to let his boss down.

"Are you listening to me?" she asked after a moment.

"Yeah, sure. Haunted house. We're checking it out. Routine stuff. In and out in twenty minutes. No problem."

She eyed him skeptically. "Is everything all right? You seem a bit distracted."

He pushed a reasonable facsimile of a smile onto his face. "I appreciate your concern." He concentrated on the road ahead. "So is it true?"

"What?"

"You're quitting PARA? Heading to the Big Apple?"

She closed her notebook and slid it back into her bag. "It's true."

"When are you through?"

"This is my last field assignment." She gazed out of the passenger-side window. "Patrick says they're throwing me a going-away party Tuesday, so I get to say goodbye to everyone. I'm going to miss them all so much. But other than that and packing, I should be out of here the day after."

Less than a week. The thought that she was leaving soon should have given him a sense of relief, but it didn't. Not even close. In fact, it made his stomach twist unpleasantly at the thought that he'd probably never see her again.

It made no sense to him at all. Why did he give a damn

either way? The woman could barely stand to be in the same car as him.

Holding on to that thought should have made things much simpler.

No such luck.

2

"GREAT WEATHER we're having, isn't it?" Jacob said tightly an hour and a half into the drive. It was the first thing he'd said for over forty-five minutes.

Amanda smiled and nodded. "June is my favorite month."

She stared out of the window but there was nothing to see in the darkness except the side of the highway racing past. A quick check of her watch told her it was nearly ten-thirty. She'd attempted to make notes in her notebook, but it was too dark, and having Jacob so close to her made it hard for her to concentrate.

He wore black jeans and a gray T-shirt that bared his strong forearms and muscled biceps, the thin material molding to his body so she could practically count his six-pack abs underneath.

Not that she was looking, of course.

She bit her bottom lip and studied the boring view out the window and thought about her boyfriend David. A wonderfully normal, respectable man with whom she'd never had one single argument.

It was his suggestion that she leave her job at PARA to work for him in the New York City office. He'd given her a choice, one that she'd never had before. She could continue living the life of Amanda the Strange—her words, not his—or she could have a chance to be Amanda the Normal.

Starting over in a fresh city with David never knowing about her psychic abilities meant she'd be consciously turning her back on her old life.

Which also, unfortunately but necessarily, included her friends, like Vicky, who didn't understand why Amanda was so adamant about making this major change in her life.

When she moved to the city she would turn off the part of her brain that allowed her to communicate with ghosts and sense other supernatural presences. She wouldn't use her abilities at all. She hoped that, over time, they'd fade away to nothing.

Her mother would be thrilled. Amanda had yet to share this news with Madeleine Harper—the last name taken from her new husband—who lived three hours south and rarely saw her daughter. She still blamed Amanda, even after all these years, for her first husband's decision to abandon their family.

Which was understandable. Even after nearly twenty years, Amanda still blamed herself.

Moving is the right thing to do, she reminded herself for the millionth time. Even so, there was the smallest piece of herself, buried down very, very deep that wasn't so sure this was the ultimate key to happiness. That piece was small enough to repress, so that's what she did. In five little days she'd be leaving Mystic Ridge for good, and she wouldn't look back.

"You can always change your mind," Jacob said.

She blinked and turned to face him. "Pardon me?"

"If you change your mind about quitting, I'm sure Patrick would be okay with that."

His comment had thrown her a bit. He couldn't know what she was thinking, could he? No, of course not. Obviously he was just trying to make conversation and the subject of her resigning from PARA was the obvious choice.

"I won't change my mind," she said firmly.

"So when you make a decision you stick to it, no matter what?"

"That's right."

"Yeah, well, I'm sure there are dozens of people who'd love to have your job, so Patrick won't have a problem finding a suitable replacement for you."

The thought that she might be so easily substituted hurt a little. "I'm sure he won't."

Jacob focused on the road ahead, but his brow lowered into a frown. "I'm just saying that if you're doing this so your new boyfriend will accept you, then that's a pretty lousy reason to turn your life upside down."

He'd been talking to somebody who had extremely loose lips. But who?

Of course, she thought with annoyance. *Vicky.*

Vicky had wanted to get Jacob alone and naked since he'd started at PARA and she'd managed to land an official date with him last month. She'd had a smile on her face for days and it was all Amanda could do to avoid hearing the sordid details of Jacob's sexual prowess.

The stab she'd felt in her gut when her best friend had informed her about the date had *not* meant she was jealous. The thought of Vicky running her hands all over Jacob's admittedly perfect body didn't bother her at all. Because that would be ridiculous. They were both consenting, condom-carrying adults, after all, and it *was* a free country.

She did know Jacob hadn't called Vicky back for a

second date. And that news hadn't been met with any relief or happiness on Amanda's part. How petty would that be?

Frankly, she didn't want to know the details of anyone's sex life—*especially* Jacob Caine's. The point was, Vicky had obviously gossiped to Jacob—before, after or during their tryst—about Amanda's situation.

"I'm *not* turning my life upside down," she said as firmly as she could. "This has nothing to do with David. It's my decision."

He gave her a sideways glance. "Sure it is."

"You don't think I can make my own decisions in life?"

"All I know is that a woman who is obviously gifted in ways that can help other people is giving up her God-given talents to go hock advertising at her boyfriend's agency and leaving behind her friends and everything she's ever known."

Hock advertising? He made it sound so unpleasant.

Jacob was trying to unnerve her and she'd be damned if she let him know he could succeed so easily.

"I'm happy with my decision," she said with resolve. "Thrilled, in fact. It's what I want."

"I don't think it is."

"You," she forced herself to smile at him, "are entitled to your opinion."

He eyed her. "Do you do that with everyone?"

The smile remained. "Do what?"

"Put on that false exterior? Do you even realize you're doing it? Maybe you don't. Maybe this is just how you always are. I wouldn't know since you've avoided me from the moment we met, so we've never really gotten a chance to get to know each other."

"I don't avoid you," she said.

He laughed. "Are you serious?"

"Our paths rarely cross at the office, sure, but it doesn't mean that I'm avoiding you. That doesn't make any sense. I barely even know you."

"If that's true, then I'm not exactly sure why you hate my guts."

Why were they having this discussion? She felt trapped, which, since they were speeding along the highway at seventy miles an hour, was quite accurate. "I don't hate you."

"Sure you do."

She shifted uncomfortably in her seat. "Why can't this drive be nice and relaxing without any conflict?"

"Good question. I guess now that I know you're definitely leaving, I'm kind of curious about everything." He took his attention off the road again long enough to look at her long and hard. "Even though you have those walls up and I can't get an empathic read on you, I can still see the truth. You might be able to pull the wool over everyone else's eyes, but you can't lie to me."

Her face felt warm. She hated how he seemed to know her so well. But he didn't. He didn't know her at all. "Is that so?"

"Yeah, that's so."

"Then I guess we're even, because I can read you like a book. I know exactly what you're thinking, Jacob, and your opinion means nothing to me."

The words hung heavily in the air between them as they studied each other for a long moment.

Then he snorted. "You're still lying. You can't read my mind. If you could, I don't think you'd like what I'm thinking."

His gaze flicked to the road for a second and then moved down the front of her, lingering at her breasts, then moving to her legs and back up again. While making her extremely self-conscious, his rude and blatant appraisal also made her nipples harden and heat spread across her skin. She felt a strange ache inside her and suddenly realized it was difficult for her to breathe normally.

She focused on his hands holding tightly to the steering wheel and in her imagination they were holding on to her, skimming her bare skin, pulling away her lacy bra to squeeze her taut nipples while his mouth took hers.

She rolled down the window a crack to get some fresh air and then cleared her throat. "I'm not lying."

"You are. It's obvious. Do you lie to David, too?"

"I'm not having this conversation with you."

His lips quirked. "Why? Does it make you uncomfortable?"

"Yes, actually it does."

"I met David once in passing when he came by the office looking for you. Seemed like a real stand-up kind of guy."

"If you mean that he's honest and reliable, then yes, he is."

"Sounds exciting."

She bit her bottom lip. "I guess compared to having fifty one-night stands already this year, my life doesn't sound that great, but I don't really care what you think."

"Fifty?" He raised an eyebrow. "Why, Miss LaGrange, I had no idea you were keeping track for me."

Her face now blazed with heat. "I'm not."

"I don't think it's fifty yet. Low-forties, maybe." He grinned. "Then again, we're only halfway through the year, aren't we?"

Great, she was amusing him. That hadn't exactly been her goal. What was her goal, again? She wanted to go to the allegedly haunted house, assess it for the presence of supernatural activity and get the hell out of there. None of which had anything to do with Jacob or his sexual conquests. She should have simply refused the assignment. Patrick would have found somebody else. The property owner could have waited a day or two with no harm done as long as she stayed out of the house.

"When you leave, who's going to keep count of the bevy of beautiful women I apparently have at my beck and call?" Jacob continued. "I'll have to buy one of those click-counter devices." He was silent for a blissful moment. "Maybe you're looking for a boring commitment from David, but that's never been what I've been looking for."

"I'm sure your ex-fiancée would be interested to hear that," she said evenly.

His expression froze. "What did you say?"

"Your *ex-fiancée,*" Amanda repeated. "Before you met her you were not the ladies' man you are now. During your three-year relationship you were completely monogamous. It's only after she left that you've become this macho, no-need-for-commitment Lothario."

She'd thrown out her knowledge of his past as a diversion to move away from her own issues and it looked as though it had worked, although not exactly in the way she'd intended. Even in the darkness of the car's interior she could tell that his face had paled at the mention of his ex.

When a new member of PARA was being recruited, extensive research was done on individuals who exhibited psychic abilities. Jacob had been pegged as a potential candidate and his life thoroughly investigated to make sure he had no ties to crime or other dark and nefarious forces. Amanda had handled the paperwork. If she had a choice, working within the agency was her preferred gig, rather than field assignments that forced her to tap into her hated abilities. That's how she knew that he'd had a broken engagement before moving to Mystic Ridge to take the job. She also knew the cause of the break-up was that his fiancée had been unfaithful to him.

She'd always assumed that, based on his lifestyle, it hadn't bothered him, but from his current expression she had to reassess that opinion. The breakup had been a bad one for him and it obviously still hurt. The pain in his eyes made her immediately regret saying anything at all.

Her stomach twisted in automatic sympathy for his pain. "I'm sorry. I...I didn't mean to bring up bad memories for you."

"My personal life is none of your damn business." The words were spoken softly but there was a sharp edge of anger behind them.

"Nor is mine yours," she said simply, fighting the feeling of guilt she now had.

"Understood."

Their eyes met and held.

The sound of a horn a few seconds later, loud and ear-shattering, made her jump, and a quick glance out of the windshield revealed a large set of oncoming headlights. She screamed and Jacob clamped down on the steering wheel to lurch the car away from the middle of the road. The transport truck that had nearly crashed into them continued to honk its horn as if to remind them how very close they'd come to a head-on collision. Jacob pulled off the road onto the side, his chest moving in and out. Amanda's heart slammed against her rib cage.

Then she realized that Jacob had put his hand on her thigh in a protective motion. His firm touch seared through her jeans and into her skin. If he slid his hand up only a few more inches...

She swallowed hard and her heart began to beat even faster than before.

"Are you okay?" he asked.

She nodded shakily. "Are you?"

The scent of his aftershave filled her senses; the rush of almost crashing, almost dying, the feel of his hand on her thigh made things low in her body ache with a dark and dangerous need she wasn't used to. His hand tightened on her leg, moving a fraction toward her inner thigh. He looked down at where he was touching her as if surprised she wasn't slapping his hand away from such intimate contact.

There was no way he couldn't see her nipples now pressing against the thin fabric of her cashmere sweater. As if he again read her thoughts, his gaze moved to her chest and he began to stroke her thigh with his thumb. It was all she could do to stop herself from arching against his touch and begging him to kiss her.

Then, suddenly, he released her. "Sorry," he said gruffly. "I need to keep my eyes on the road. That's never happened before. I must be tired."

"It's fine," she managed.

He pulled the car back onto the road. "We're almost there, anyhow. Like you said, twenty minutes to check it out, and then we can leave."

"Good."

She pressed back into the seat and studied the road ahead, her body still tingling where Jacob had touched her.

3

It was obvious to him now, after nearly slamming head-on into a transport truck. His continuing attraction to Amanda was going to kill him.

Literally.

It was a good thing they'd never been partnered before. He'd probably already be dead. The raging hard-on he was currently dealing with alone might kill him.

Jacob shook his head, silently chastising himself. Amanda had her own life. She was moving three hundred miles away and good riddance to her. He much preferred to be fully in charge of his emotions, and, for that matter, his *cock*.

He did find it more than a little interesting that she seemed to have taken an interest in his sex life. Fifty one-night stands? That was one hell of an overestimation. When he needed to let some steam off he rarely had any problems finding somebody willing to help him out, but *fifty?*

Hell, most nights he stayed home with a six-pack of Bud and the Playboy channel. Sad but true, lately it gave him almost as much satisfaction as the real thing. He'd definitely hit a slump. Two years since his big break-up and move to Mystic Ridge and he hadn't found a single woman that interested him enough to see more than once.

Obviously the fault was with him. He knew it. He just wasn't quite ready to deal with that yet.

"We're here," he said after what seemed like an eternity of silence between them. It had really only been a half hour since the brush with death...and the distracting contact with Amanda's jeans-clad thigh.

He pulled into the driveway of the house set on a large lot. The house itself looked to be at least a hundred years old and the drive was flanked by thick oak trees that would have made the area dark even at noon.

Another car—a silver Volkswagen Jetta—idled in front of them and as soon as they pulled up a small woman with curly red hair, lit by Jacob's headlights, stepped out of it. She beckoned them to join her.

"Guess we're on the clock already," Jacob said.

"Then let's get it over with," Amanda replied curtly. She quickly gathered her paperwork together, opened the passenger-side door, and got out.

Let's get it over with. For some reason the phrase amused him. Was that how she might view a hot night of sex with her true love, David K. Smith?

"Let's get it over with, honey."

Sounded about right.

Pushing any thoughts of Amanda and sex out of his head, Jacob got out of the car to join his partner-of-the-moment in front of the irate-looking woman.

"I've been waiting for an hour already," she snapped.

Jacob tensed at the shrill, impatient tone. He was about to open his mouth to say something, probably along the lines of "Chill out, lady, we're here now," when Amanda beat him to the punch.

"We apologize for any inconvenience, Mrs. Davis—"

"It's *Ms.* Davis."

What a huge surprise, Jacob thought dryly.

"*Ms.* Davis," Amanda repeated, and then smiled warmly at the unpleasant woman. "But we did get here as soon as we could. This location is a fair drive for us."

"That's no excuse."

Jacob was surprised that Amanda's smile held. Hell, if he'd given her this much of a problem she'd be giving him the death glare by now.

Her death glare *was* kind of cute.

Amanda's smile, though, did weaken a bit at the edges as she juggled her papers. She loved paperwork. He knew that. However, he hadn't been aware that some of the paperwork she'd handled had to do with him and his past. It had made him more than a little uncomfortable when she'd brought up the subject of his ex-fiancée.

Served him right. She'd only been giving him a very big sign to stay away from her personal issues. It was only fair.

Best to keep things just business between them. No personal issues need apply.

Still, it bothered him. He would have rather kept up the facade of an unrepentant ladies' man than some fool still nursing a broken heart.

Besides, he wasn't nursing that broken heart anymore. He'd thrown it away. That's what you did with broken things. You got rid of them so they didn't cause unnecessary clutter.

A few pages from Amanda's stack came loose and fluttered to the ground. She grabbed at them as Ms. Davis raised an eyebrow.

"Let's move this along, dear. I don't have all night."

Amanda's face flushed. Jacob leaned over and picked

up some of the fallen pages and handed them back to her. She looked frustrated.

It was okay. He'd handle this.

"Ms. Davis," he said out loud, turning toward the short redhead and giving her one of his very best smiles. He extended his hand to her. "I'm Jacob Caine."

She hesitated for a brief moment, and then shook his hand.

That was all he needed. The skin-to-skin contact helped him get an empathic read on her. She obviously had no psychic abilities. Since joining PARA, he'd found that some psychics, such as Amanda, were a blank page to him. This woman on the other hand was wide open. He got the immediate impression she was equal parts lonely and needy.

He could *totally* work with that.

He squeezed her hand before letting it go. "What I want to know is why a beautiful woman like yourself would want to live in such a dreary house like this. I see you in a high-rise condo in a big city. Very cosmopolitan."

Her thin eyebrows raised. "You're a very good psychic. I actually have an offer in on a new complex in Chicago as we speak."

"The perfect city," he said. "I'm actually from Chicago originally myself. I moved away from there two years ago."

"Really?"

He nodded. Well, to be quite honest, he was from Seattle, but that wouldn't help at all at the moment. White lies for the right reasons were totally acceptable.

"This is Amanda LaGrange." He nodded toward the beautiful brunette next to him who regarded him with a bemused expression as he worked his own personal kind of magic. A magic he liked to call *natural charm*. "She already has the details of your case, but I think it would be best if we hear it from you in your own words."

His attention returned to Ms. Davis, whose expression had changed to a very pleased one. She liked him. A smile, a few complimentary words, and he was in.

Between the two women in his current company, Ms. Davis wouldn't be his first choice, but he did like that glow he'd set into her cheeks. He'd rather see that glow on Amanda's face when she looked at him, but knew that was going to happen exactly...*never.*

Ms. Davis turned to the old, stone-faced house with ivy crawling up the front. To Jacob it looked creepy, but he supposed some might find a certain charm in it.

"My house is infested with evil spirits," she stated. "And I want them gone."

"Evil spirits?" Jacob repeated.

Amanda shuffled through her papers. "It says here that last night you heard noises and had the sensation of being pushed out of certain rooms. I'm not sure that counts as a supernatural infestation."

Ms. Davis's eyes narrowed. "Are you doubting what I said is true?"

"Of course not, I'm just saying—"

Jacob held up his hand. "We'll check it out. Don't worry, Ms. Davis...may I call you Sheila?"

Her sour expression turned into a smile. "You may."

"Please tell me more about the evil spirits, Sheila."

She ran a hand through her red curls as if grooming herself for inspection. "My uncle left me this house but I want to get rid of it. One can't very well have an open house for potential buyers if there are evil forces at work. Haunted houses are curious tourist attractions, but ghosts are not exactly something that raises one's property value."

"I totally and completely agree." Jacob glanced at Amanda who rolled her eyes. "We will handle this, I personally promise you that."

She beamed at him. "I'll be staying at the Marriott. I expect a full report first thing in the morning."

"And you'll have it."

"Very good." Sheila eyed Amanda. "You're very lucky to have a boss like Jacob taking the lead. I can tell he knows what to do."

Her blue eyes widened. "But he's not my—"

Jacob interrupted. "It was a pleasure meeting you, Sheila. And you can expect my call bright and early. Sleep well, now."

He opened her car door for her and Sheila got inside.

"Be careful in there," she told him.

"I'll do my best."

Jacob eased the door shut and after another moment, Sheila drove off down the driveway leaving the two of them alone.

"She thought you were my boss," Amanda said.

"It must be my air of authority."

"I don't think it was necessary to flirt with her."

"You don't think so?" He raised an eyebrow. "What can I say? It comes so naturally. There are very few women who can resist me."

Amanda looked as if she wanted to smile at that, but restrained herself. "Right. Well, let's get this over with."

Without another word, she turned away and marched up to the front door of Sheila Davis's allegedly haunted house.

THE HOUSE was definitely haunted. No doubt about it. Amanda felt the presence as soon as she stepped inside.

"Grab the lights," she told Jacob. He complied and flicked on the nearest overhead light and the front foyer was bathed in a warm, golden glow.

The house was gorgeous. It reminded Amanda of her grandfather's house—the man she'd never got to see again after her father abandoned them. She used to play in that house as a kid and, in fact, it was where she'd encountered her first ghost.

She stroked her hand along the smooth wall. There was definitely a spirit here. Amanda frowned. No. She could sense *more* than one spirit haunting this house. But she wasn't able to tell yet if they were going to be a problem or not.

"You okay?" Jacob asked.

She was surprised by the concern that edged his words. It made her realize that she'd closed her eyes and pressed both her hands flat up against the wall. A thin sheen of perspiration glazed her forehead from concentrating.

Yeah, that must have looked really normal.

Amanda the Strange rides again.

She self-consciously wiped a hand across her brow. "I'm fine."

"What were you doing?"

Since they hadn't worked together before, Jacob hadn't witnessed the weird trance she tended to go into when she tapped fully into her abilities. It was one of the many reasons she preferred office work. She hated how using her "powers" made her lose control of herself, even if only a little.

She waved a hand dismissively. "Just...you know. I was sensing if there was any ghostly activity."

"And?"

She eyed him. "You're psychic, too."

"Yeah, but empaths are different. I get my glimpses through touching somebody alive, like little Miss Attitude outside. I don't normally get sent on these kinds of assignments. Obviously Patrick was really stuck tonight. You're the only ghost whisperer here."

"I do sense something."

"Yeah?" His eyebrows went up. "So fast? What is it?"

"There are a couple of ghosts here."

He glanced around the immediate surroundings. "Can you see them?"

"No. Not yet. But they're here." She drew in a sharp breath. "A male and a female. They were—" she paused, sinking deeper into her strange ability so she could get a better sense of the place "—involved in some way romantically. Not husband and wife, but *lovers,* I think."

"You can tell that just from touching the wall?"

She pulled her hand back and cleared her throat. "Well, it's just the vibe I'm getting. Maybe I'm wrong."

After a moment when he didn't say anything, she glanced at him cautiously. "What?"

He shook his head. "It's just kind of amazing to me. I've been on assignment with lots of other agents, but you're different from them, aren't you?"

She crossed her arms. "You can save the judgment for another time."

"Judgment?"

"I feel self-conscious enough about what I have to do without you making me feel bad about it."

He blinked. "You're serious, aren't you? Are you actually trying to pick a fight with me about this? We just got here."

"And we're almost done."

When people studied what she could do too closely it made her feel like a sideshow freak. Echoes of "Amanda the Strange" went through her head and she cringed.

"Let's check out the rest of the house quickly." She moved away down the hall but his strong, warm hand encircled her upper arm to stop her.

"Wait a second, Amanda."

She slowly turned to look at Jacob who now had an odd look on his face.

"What?"

"You have a problem."

"Tell me something I don't know. That's why I want to go to New York. I want to be normal."

He just looked at her incredulously. "You seriously think that, don't you? That you're not normal."

She shrugged his hand away. "It's not normal to connect with the supernatural world. It's creepy and wrong."

He had a deep frown on his face now. "Who told you something like that?"

"Everybody."

"Everybody? I find that very hard to believe."

"My mother never approved of what I could do. In fact, she hated it. She made sure I knew on a daily basis it was abnormal and unnatural and freakish. And at school..." She trailed off. "Look, I don't want to talk about this right now, okay? I know it's strange and just because I can do it doesn't mean I like it."

He laughed then. At her. She felt heat come to her cheeks.

"Fine, laugh," she said tightly. "I'm used to that."

"You're completely crazy, you know that?"

"I'm not crazy."

"I think I'd have to disagree with that."

She let out a sigh of frustration. "You don't know me."

"I think I do. And I'll tell you why I think I know you. Because you think that after that little psychic display I think you're a freak. I can't believe your mother would say that to you." He seemed actually angry about it.

"Forget it."

He cocked his head to the side. "You're all ruffled now. Lost that cool composure from before, huh? Do I really have the ability to make you lose control of yourself?"

"I really think I hate you."

He snorted. "Now it's hate. Awesome. Before, I knew it was indifference, maybe a little bit of disgust, but hate is so much more interesting."

"Why are you baiting me like this?"

"Because I don't think anybody ever does bait you like this. Nobody challenges you, Amanda. Nobody pushes your buttons."

"Maybe I don't want my buttons pushed."

He raised a dark eyebrow. "Maybe your buttons have never been pushed by the right person."

Her cheeks grew warmer. "Let's leave my buttons out of this."

"I don't think that's possible." His gaze slid down her front and she self-consciously crossed her arms as a feeble form of protection from his intense scrutiny. "What you can do is amazing. *You're* amazing, whether you realize it or not."

"Amazing," she said the word with an ironic twist. "So amazing that my father was freaked out by me and abandoned my family when I was a kid and my mom was stuck raising me."

His eyes narrowed. "He did that?"

"A ghost pushed him down the stairs. He kind of blamed me for that."

"He blamed *you?*" Another flash of anger entered his gaze.

"Of course he did. It was my fault the ghost was there in the first place."

She turned away from him wishing the heat would leave her face. But there was something about Jacob that definitely did push those hidden buttons of hers. Why did she let him get to her? What was it about this admittedly gorgeous jerk that totally flustered her?

"You want him to make love to you so badly you can barely remain standing, don't you?"

She frowned at the thought, not to mention the mental images it invoked.

Then her eyes went very wide. She hadn't just thought that. She'd *heard* it. Somebody had spoken those words to her.

She looked at Jacob, who was frowning at her sudden change in expression.

"What is it?" The concern returned to his green eyes as if he sensed something had changed.

Something had.

"Um..." she began. "I was right. This house is definitely haunted."

"What? You can see the ghost?"

She nodded.

"Where is it?" he asked.

She swallowed hard. "Standing right next to you."

4

LEANING AGAINST the wall was a beautiful ghost with long blond hair, wearing a long white gown. Amanda could tell it was a ghost because she could see right through to the wall behind her.

"You heard me?" the ghost asked.

Amanda studied the woman for a moment. "I heard you."

The ghost glanced at Jacob. "He's very handsome. I can see why you're attracted to him."

"What's happening?" Jacob asked, scanning the area around him. "I can't see anything."

The ghost walked slowly around Jacob, checking him out from head to toe and pausing at all the key places—his broad shoulders, muscled arms and chest, firm ass and the hard-to-ignore bulge at the front of his jeans.

Amanda's mouth wasn't dry anymore.

"Uh...Amanda..." Jacob snapped her out of her sudden daze. "Why are you looking at me like that? Where's the ghost now?"

Get a grip, she told herself sternly. This was not the time or place to flake out.

You want him to make love to you so badly you can barely remain standing.

Was that what the ghost had said?

So not true. She wasn't obsessed with sex. She didn't fixate on the physical—no matter how perfect a subject Jacob might be.

Stupid ghost.

"What's your name?" Amanda asked.

The beautiful woman tore her appraising gaze away from Jacob's body and looked at her. "My name is Catherine. This is my house. Or at least it used to be. Why are you here?"

Amanda rubbed her dry lips together. "We're here to ask you to leave this house, and we hope you'll be open to that suggestion. Do you know what keeps you bound here?"

"This is the only place we can be together," Catherine replied, and there was sadness in her expression now.

"Are you open to leaving?"

"No. This is where we belong. Where we must stay. There is no other choice for us."

Amanda scanned the area. Jacob had taken a step back, watching curiously as she spoke to the ghost he couldn't see. "Where is the other ghost?"

"Right here." A man walked directly out of the wall next to where Amanda stood. He was tall and handsome, with dark-blond hair and blue eyes. His gaze, though, was anything but friendly. The glare he directed at Amanda made chills run down her arms. "You need to leave us in peace."

Catherine looked at the man and there was no doubting the affection in her eyes. "Nathan, please. I can handle this."

He stiffened then turned to face her. "I only get to see you for an hour a day. I don't want our time interrupted by these intruders."

Her brows drew together. "I know. But it's dangerous."

His jaw tensed. "It's always been dangerous for us."

Then he reached out toward Catherine and she did the same. When their hands came within two feet of each other a flash of light appeared and the ghosts disappeared. At the same time, what felt like a bolt of electricity ripped through Amanda and she gasped out loud. Her knees buckled. She was sure she'd fall to the floor, but Jacob was there to catch her, keeping her on her feet.

"They're cursed," she managed after a moment. Her eyelids fluttered and she realized she may have blacked out for a moment. "The ghosts—they were involved romantically when they were alive, but couldn't be together. They died at the same time, I think. Now they're bound in this house together, but they can only see each other for short periods and they can't touch."

"Did they tell you this?" Jacob asked, his forehead creased deeply.

She shook her head. "I had a vision just now. It was blurry and disjointed but it was sort of like I was actually there, seeing with my own eyes what happened." She inhaled sharply. "How horrible to be like that. To be able to be with the one you love but never touch each other."

"Cursed spirits," Jacob said. "Sounds like an exorcism is definitely required here."

His arms were still around her and the hard line of his body pressing against hers was enough to pull her back to reality—mostly because it felt too good. "I'm okay now. You can let go of me."

He released her immediately. "Sorry."

She fumbled through her bag and pulled out a notebook in which she scribbled down as much as she could remember of her sudden vision of the two ghosts. She didn't normally see with such clarity. Sure, she could see the ghost itself, talk to it, and try to come to some sort of an understanding. Sometimes the ghost could be convinced to leave the mortal world through a simple conversation. Exorcism was a worst-case scenario.

But visions were new. One more ability to add to her unwelcome repertoire. *Great.*

Maybe Nathan had murdered Catherine and then killed himself. Was that why they were being punished? She wasn't sure. She'd only seen glimpses. Some kind of magic had been involved here.

It didn't matter. The bottom line was they'd confirmed ghostly activity in the house and the owner wanted that taken care of.

The ghosts hadn't been violent, which was good. But that sense of despair and desperation to touch each other—

A chill went through her.

"I know I haven't been much help so far," Jacob said. "Sorry about that."

She looked up to see his forehead was furrowed. "Forget it. You can't see what I see."

"Unfortunately."

"Don't say that. It's not all it's cracked up to be."

"Says you." He sighed. "To be able to do what you do? That's a gift."

"Curse."

"Gift."

She forced a tight smile on her face. "I guess we'll have to agree to disagree on that point."

He didn't try to argue any more about that, which was a nice change. She couldn't help but smile inwardly at his reaction. Most of the other PARA agents Amanda had been teamed up with over the years had a very matter-of-fact way of dealing with the unusual stuff. Like it was normal for them. Average. Almost boring.

Jacob looked at it as though it was *amazing*. Then again he'd only discovered his psychic abilities a couple of years ago. He hadn't had to deal with them for decades.

Curse. Definitely.

They moved through the living room and Amanda pulled at a corner of the plastic covering the sofa.

"I think this sofa is original," she said. "Well over a hundred years old."

"*Antiques Roadshow* would have a field day in here."

She ran her fingers lightly over the dark material underneath. More images came to her mind and she gasped.

"Hey," Jacob said. "Are you getting something?"

She nodded. "Definitely something."

"What is it?"

"I don't...I don't know yet..." She tried to see past the fog, worried she was going in too deep and beginning to pull away, but the vision was suddenly there in front of her again, this time as clear as day.

Catherine was leading Nathan into the room. He was reluctant to follow but helpless to her charms. He found her so beautiful; too beautiful to resist, even though she was the wife of his employer. Ever since the other night at midnight when they'd first made love, he had been unable to think of anyone else.

"This isn't right," he murmured in a feeble attempt to stop her.

"Shh," she silenced him with another kiss.

"Your husband—"

"Please, Nathan...I want you so much..."

Her hands found the buttons on his pants and she undid

them one by one until she freed his erection. As she slid her tongue along his length he was completely helpless to her.

He loved her with all his heart and soul. He knew he didn't deserve her, but wanted to be with her like this always. Every time they made love was better than the last. The feel of her body clenching him as he drove into her, his hands on her breasts, his mouth swirling over the peaks of her nipples as he thrust himself into her slick heat—

"Amanda—" she heard Jacob say from a million miles away, but she couldn't drag herself out of the vision, her body on fire as she sank into the deep, warm pool of passion from memories that didn't belong to her. The vision was of bodies moving together, gasps and soft moans, as Catherine and Nathan made love.

A clock chimed. Twelve times. It was midnight.

It was significant, that clock. Amanda tried to focus on it—a large black grandfather clock with an ivory face that stood against the wall.

Catherine let out a soft cry, arching her back, her breasts flattening against Nathan's hard-muscled chest as he brought her to orgasm.

And then a blur. A flash. And they were apart. It was later, but Amanda couldn't tell how much later. The clock was now obscured by the shape of a man. A murderously jealous husband. Words were spoken, threats and curses thrown out.

"You'll never touch her again."

There was the sharp crack of several gunshots. Catherine's scream of pain and terror. A fight. Nathan's furious, grief-filled gaze stilled by another shot.

The glass on the front of the clock was shattered by a stray bullet.

Two nude bodies were found by the police. Lovers. A suicide pact, the police decided. The husband claimed ignorance and dark grief that his slut of a wife would take up with a common servant. A nobody.

Catherine and Nathan were bound to the house where they were murdered, but unable to see each other except for one hour a day, from eleven o'clock to midnight. When the chimes of the clock grew silent, they'd disappear from each other's view, never able to touch each other.

But why? Why were they still trapped there?

Amanda let out a shaky sob as she finally came out of the vision and realized she was crying. She also realized that somebody held her tightly in his arms while seated on the floor—it was Jacob.

"Amanda, can you hear me?" He wiped away her tears with his thumbs as he held her face gently between his hands. "Are you okay?"

"I'm fine. I...I just got a little carried away there."

"I see that."

He stroked the hair that had come loose from her ponytail back from her face. His touch was electric and she took a sharp inhalation of breath. Her body still felt the aftereffects of the lust-filled vision, her skin more sensitive than normal. Hot to the touch. She braced her hands against his firm chest to try to push him away but didn't. He felt so good pressed against her.

Much too good.

"What time is it?" she asked.

"Quarter to twelve."

When the clock struck midnight Catherine and Nathan couldn't see each other until the next day. For eternity. Maybe it would be an act of kindness to have them exorcised. She couldn't imagine, after seeing the sadness in their eyes, that this existence was a happy one for them.

Dammit. She hated her job sometimes.

No, not sometimes. Despite her friends and the generous paycheck, she *always* hated her job. In her new life with David, she wouldn't have to deal with cursed ghost lovers and chiming clocks that kept them apart.

Chiming clocks.

The clock had taken up a good part of her vision. That had to have some significance. Could it be possible that it had something to do with the curse? It seemed to revolve around time, after all.

Still seated on the floor with Jacob, Amanda glanced off to the side to see Catherine standing watching her. Nathan was nowhere to be seen.

"Please, you must go," Catherine said. "We mean no harm. Leave us in peace."

"Where's the clock?" Amanda asked.

"The clock?"

"The big black grandfather clock." Amanda looked around the room. "It was once there, in that corner, but now it's gone. Where is it?"

Catherine shook her head. "You shouldn't bother with that. It's dangerous."

"Dangerous?"

"The clock is enchanted. It was given to me by my aunt, a self-proclaimed witch, as a wedding gift. She never approved of my marriage, said that a marriage where there was no love was doomed." She set her chin. "I guess she was right about that. The clock works its magic at midnight and is the reason Nathan and I are in this situation in the first place. Why we're bound to this house and to each other forever."

Amanda shook her head. "But we deal with enchanted objects, especially dangerous ones. I need to assess it. Maybe we can help you."

Her attention moved to the other side of the room where Nathan had reappeared.

"The clock is upstairs," he said. "You should definitely go see it."

"Nathan," Catherine said sharply.

He cocked his head to the side. "I'm only trying to help them."

"Why do you have to interfere? This is none of our business."

Nathan's gaze was intense. "If it weren't for the clock, we wouldn't be together."

Amanda could sense Jacob staring as her head turned from side to side as if she was watching a tennis match. She felt as though she was. One that didn't make any sense to her.

"I have to say it's a bit unnerving not knowing what's going on right in front of my own eyes," he said.

"Help me up," she whispered.

Jacob got up and offered her his hand. She took it and he pulled her to her feet.

"The ghosts?" he asked.

She scanned the room. They'd disappeared the moment she turned away from them.

She ran through the information she'd received. Catherine's aunt had given her the clock as a wedding gift and Catherine believed it to be enchanted in some way—the reason her and Nathan's spirits were trapped in the house.

It was almost midnight. If she could witness what happened when the clock struck midnight, maybe that would help in the assessment. If she could do something, anything to break the curse for the ghosts...

Why was she allowing herself to become so involved with this? She didn't even like love stories, let alone tragic ones that ended in murder.

"The ghosts are gone," she said. "For now. We need to find the clock."

"What clock?"

What was she supposed to say to that that didn't make her sound completely insane? Then again, what did she care what Jacob thought of her? "It's a clock that was here when the ghosts were cursed. It might even be the cause of the curse. We need to find it, assess it, and then we're getting out of here."

"The last part's the best suggestion I've heard all evening."

"Do you have a camera?"

"Yeah, right here." He patted his pocket.

There was a stairway at the end of the hall. The lights were dim and not all of them worked but it was enough to see their way. Amanda wasn't afraid. Some might be in a haunted house, but she'd already met the ghosts. Not the friendliest sort, but nothing overtly evil there.

She'd felt their love. She'd seen it in the vision. It hadn't been only an affair, it had been deeper, truer. Not everyone found that sort of love in their life. But if it made one make dangerous and questionable decisions that led to getting shot, then she'd prefer to keep to the much more orderly emotions, thanks.

There was no chance that her relationship with David would end up with her pining away for his spirit. Not that she didn't care for him; there was some strong affection there, but *love?*

Amanda's life was unpredictable enough dealing with her psychic abilities without adding love to the equation.

"WHY DO we care about this clock, again?" Jacob asked as they ascended the staircase to the second floor of the dimly lit, musty-smelling house.

Amanda didn't answer right away, which worried him a little. Was she in another trance? Was she communicating with the ghosts? He'd never worked with her before, but he'd worked with other mediums enough to know that dead people weren't always friendly and cooperative. No, sometimes they were vicious and violent and intent on possession. A soft, sweet-smelling, warm human body like Amanda's would be their first choice to thrust themselves into.

That wasn't supposed to be a sexy thought, Jacob chastised himself as his cock stiffened at the mental image. Just when he'd thought he'd gotten himself under control again.

Damn.

He grabbed her arm and made her stop halfway up the stairs. "Hey. You okay?"

Her face was paler than it had been before. She blinked and seemed to focus on him. "Yeah, I'm fine. Why are you looking at me like that?"

"Like what?"

"Like you're worried."

"Probably because I am."

That made a small smile appear on those disconcertingly kissable lips of hers. "You're worried about me?"

"Sure. There's no reason for us still to be here prodding around. We need to go back to the office and file our report."

"I never knew you were such a rule-follower."

"I'm not." He realized he was still touching her and he removed his hand, instead clenching it at his side. "But I don't want anything bad to happen."

"Nothing bad will happen. The ghosts aren't evil."

"Are you sure about that?"

"They were in love. They're cursed now and can't touch each other, can't see each other except for an hour a day. It must be hell for them. If you could see them, Jacob—"

"But I can't."

"No." She sighed with frustration. "You can't. But I can. I can see that if the curse was broken, if they could be fully together again, then they'd likely find their peace and leave the house without any drastic measures."

"Drastic measures like an exorcism."

"Exactly."

"Since when are you so against exorcisms? It's kind of what you do, isn't it?"

"Sure, if the situation calls for it. But if there's another reason, or if there's a story behind it...if we can do something to help—"

"They're already dead."

"Doesn't mean that they're not still in love."

He eyed her for a long moment before he started to laugh. The dreamy look on her face immediately vanished and was replaced by a harder edge.

"What's so damn funny?" she asked.

"You. You're a romantic. I never would have guessed it in a million years."

"I'm not a romantic."

"You want the ghosts to find their happy ending."

The look she gave him now was icy. She didn't like

having her harsh exterior prodded. He already knew that. And he was prodding. He liked prodding her a little too much. It could easily become a habit. Possibly an addiction.

"Finding the clock is not being romantic, it's doing my job," she explained evenly. "If the clock is cursed and dangerous it needs to be destroyed."

He just smiled at her. "Sure."

Her cheeks reddened. "I really think I hate you."

"Harsh words, Miss LaGrange. Has your boyfriend seen this nasty side of you?"

"He doesn't have to. I actually like him."

"*Like?* What a romantic word. I can see why you're throwing your life away to be with such a Romeo."

"Would you please shut up now?" She turned away from him and jogged the rest of the way up the stairs, succeeding in putting a bit of distance between them.

His amused buzz disappeared. What the hell was he doing, exactly? Why was he arguing about romance with this woman? Why was he filled with a sense of being alive just being in her presence? It made no sense. *Zero.* Even if there was a chance to explore something between them—something his body seemed ready for when Amanda was just in the same zip code as him—she was already taken. And she was moving away. Soon.

Stop it, he told himself sternly. *Just stop it.*

He needed a hobby. Maybe he'd start collecting stamps. Give his mind something to fixate on other than frustrating women who gladly ruined their lives for the wrong men.

They seriously needed to get out of here. It was only a few minutes before midnight, and with a two-hour drive ahead of them to get back to Mystic Ridge, he'd like to get started on that as soon as possible.

Five days, he reminded himself. Five days and she'd be gone. Forever.

The thought was supposed to make him feel better.

It didn't.

AMANDA felt compelled to find that clock. It was not as if the house was a mansion. It was large with multiple rooms on the second floor, but it wasn't as if something so large as a grandfather clock could hide from her for long.

If it weren't for the clock, we wouldn't be together, Nathan had said.

Amanda wished he'd been friendly enough to explain what that meant. Was the clock really the reason behind their curse? Why would Catherine's aunt give her something so potentially dangerous as a wedding gift? It made no sense.

They needed to take pictures of the clock and write down details. Then she'd take that information back to headquarters and do in-depth research to find out more about it and, she hoped, how to reverse whatever magic it had worked in the past.

The fact that Jacob was still following her on her wild-goose chase around the house almost amused her considering he was right to a certain degree—their work here was done. They hadn't been sent to investigate any inanimate objects, just the ghosts. And they'd finished. The ghosts refused to leave. They would be exorcised once all the paperwork was completed. A few days, tops. Then the owner of the house could be assured that her property was spirit-free.

It made sense, which was why Amanda's insistence on exploring the dark house at going on midnight was a little...what was the word?

Strange.

Ah yes, *that* word again.

She refrained from rolling her eyes at herself. For some-body hell-bent on getting away from PARA, she sure was dedicated to her job.

She glanced over her shoulder at the gorgeous man behind her. "I know this is a bit freakish."

"I wouldn't say that exactly."

Her eyebrows went up a fraction. "No?"

"You're talking to the wrong person about what is and isn't freakish. To me, this is kind of fun."

She shook her head. "You're obviously crazier than I am."

"No argument there." A sexy smile appeared on his lips that did strange things to her insides. She tried to ignore it. "So does this mean you've changed your mind about hating me?"

"I wouldn't think you'd care what I think of you one way or the other."

He shrugged. "I don't, of course. I'm just wondering."

"*Hate* is such a strong word, really. Maybe loathing or distaste mixed with apathy fits better."

"That sounds more like it." The smile slipped away and was replaced with a less-friendly, more guarded expression. "Let's find that clock."

Good plan.

The truth was, the longer Amanda was in Jacob's presence, the more she didn't dislike him, which was disturbing, to say the least. Ever since they'd first met and she'd felt that initial spark—which had been quickly extinguished when he'd used her hated nickname—she'd held on to that distaste for him. It made things a lot simpler. Cleaner.

That was how she liked life to be: clean and simple.

She heard the clock then. Its ticking was loud and precise behind the closed door in front of her. She wasn't entirely sure why the sound sent a chill of anticipation through her body.

"I think it might be in here," she said after a moment of uncomfortable silence passed between them.

"Lead the way." There was a pause, and then, "Hey, Amanda."

"What?" She looked back at him. She jumped when a flash went off. When the spots left her eyes and the hallway darkened again she glared at him. "Why did you take my picture?"

"Just making sure everything's in working order." But he looked way too smug for that to be the only reason. Baiting her. Fantastic. Glad that she amused him. Really professional behavior there. He glanced down at the view screen. "You're very photogenic, I'll give you that."

"Sure I am." She didn't want to see it. She probably looked like a pissed-off troll with the flash so close to her face. "Delete it, please."

"Yes, ma'am."

She pushed open the door in front of her to find that it led into a large bedroom. Unlike the other rooms they'd been in, this one looked all ready for the open house since there was no plastic wrap covering the furniture and it smelled fresh and pleasant, like roses and freesia, rather than musty and dusty. A canopied queen-sized bed was to one side, draped in gauzy material that blended with the hand-woven, cream-colored carpeting. A window to their left looked down to the driveway and thatch of oak trees. A glance out showed Jacob's car parked below.

Against the wall across from the door was the clock

she'd seen in her vision. Eight feet tall, black, and it stood there like a monster silently lurking in the dark.

Or maybe she was projecting. It was possible. She refused to be afraid of a stupid inanimate object.

"That's it?" Jacob asked.

She nodded.

He approached it with confidence and slid his hand up the smooth front of it. "Doesn't look all that dangerous to me."

"Be careful."

He shot her a droll look. "You *do* care about me, after all. Don't worry, I'm sure the big bad clock isn't going to hurt me."

"Don't be so sure about that. It might."

He removed his hand, then began to snap a few pictures of the clock, long shots, close-ups. And of the face itself, still showing the broken glass from where a stray bullet had hit the white surface in her vision, that currently read two minutes to midnight. The pendulum swung evenly back and forth counting off the seconds.

Amanda attempted to ignore the muscles that flexed in Jacob's arms, the way his back moved, the hard planes of his chest, how well those jeans fitted his muscled thighs and lean hips. Her attention moved to his green eyes and short dark hair and she absently wondered if it was as soft as it looked.

He eyed her. "Are you just going to gawk at me or are you going to write anything down in that notebook of yours?"

A flush came to her cheeks yet again. She wasn't gawking. Much.

Suddenly Catherine appeared next to her in a pulse of soft light.

"You must leave." The ghost cast a tense look at the clock. "It's not safe for you here."

"What are you talking about?"

"What?" Jacob asked absently.

"I'm speaking to the ghost. She's next to me right now."

"Oh...well, carry on." He continued to take pictures.

Catherine looked very stressed for a ghost. "There's no time left. It's almost midnight. My aunt's magic...the clock...you need to trust me. Go now."

"I don't understand," Amanda said. "I'm trying to help you. I'm trying to determine exactly what the problem with the clock is and I need data to take back with me—"

"Then leave this room just for now. Come back in an hour. But you can't be here when the clock strikes midnight!"

Which was less than a minute away.

"Why not?" Amanda's eyes began to widen. "What happens at midnight? I know you and Nathan will disappear."

"It's more than that. The clock's magic strips away one's ability to think and act rationally, which is what happened to myself and Nathan. We lost control."

"Lost control?" Amanda repeated.

Jacob stopped taking pictures for a moment. "Is there a problem?"

"The door to this room should have been locked." Catherine wrung her transparent hands together. "That horrible woman, the one who wants us to leave, she must have unlocked it." She swept a glance over the room and scrunched her nose with distaste. "And she's replaced the bedding. The color palette she's chosen is not attractive at all."

"Forget the colors," Amanda protested, feeling panic well inside her. "Let's get back on the topic. You want us to leave but I need to know why. It might help with our investigation. It might help *you*."

"Catherine," Nathan appeared next to her. His face was

much more serene than hers now. "Leave them be. It's fate that they're here."

"Fate." She spat the word like a curse. "Fate is what got us into this situation in the first place, isn't it?"

His lips thinned and a momentary doubt crossed his gaze as he looked at Catherine. "Do you wish it had been different for us?"

Instead of snapping at him or getting angry, her features softened as their eyes met and held. "They don't realize what this means."

"They will," Nathan whispered. "Besides, it's already too late."

"What the hell are you—?" Amanda began again, confused and deeply disturbed by the exchange she was witnessing.

The clock struck midnight.

5

CATHERINE looked upset, but Nathan looked smug as the chimes sounded out from the clock.

Amanda's eyes widened. "What's going to happen now?"

Jacob reacted to the tense tone in her voice by coming to her side, staring around at the otherwise empty room and the ghosts he couldn't see.

Nathan smiled at her. "You and your friend are as doomed as we are."

"What can we do?"

"Nothing." He glanced at Catherine's stern expression and his smile turned sadder. "Till tomorrow, my love."

"Tomorrow," she murmured as the last chime echoed through the room.

The ghosts disappeared in separate flashes of light.

Jacob and Amanda stood, frozen in place, staring at each other.

"What's happening?" Jacob asked.

"The ghosts say we're doomed," she replied, glancing at the clock which now read exactly midnight. "Oh shit."

"What?"

"The clock. It's...it's glowing..."

He looked at it to see it surrounded by a soft white light. The clock itself had frozen at the last stroke of midnight, its pendulum still. "Why the hell is it glowing?"

"Because it's midnight."

"What does that mean?"

The next moment, the glow turned into a blinding pulse of light that blanketed the entire bedroom for a split second before disappearing. The door to the room slammed shut and a thunderbolt of pain ripped through Amanda's head. She brought her hands up to her temples. Her knees buckled. Jacob caught her before she hit the ground. When she looked up into his face she found it looked as tense as she felt.

"What the hell?" he managed. "What was that?"

"I'm not exactly sure."

But there was something wrong. She could feel it down deep in her bones. She didn't have to be psychic to know that something had changed, shifted, with the clock striking midnight and the painful pulse of light. But what was it?

"Are you going to fill me in on everything Casper was saying to you or do I have to guess?" Jacob asked.

"I wish I knew." He still had his arm around her and for some reason or another she didn't immediately pull away. Better to stay this way for another moment just in case she lost her footing again. "They wanted us to clear out of this room before midnight but I guess it's a little late for that."

"Sounds ominous. There's nothing worse than vague ghosts."

She couldn't help but laugh nervously at that. Maybe she was overreacting. Maybe the spirits had been playing with her. It wouldn't be the first time she'd encountered otherworldly beings who got their fun messing with the minds of the living.

"We can leave now," she said firmly. "We have all the

research materials we need. There's definitely something strange about that clock."

"I totally agree." He was close enough that she felt the warmth from his breath brush against her cheek. The pleasant sensation was enough to cause a small wave of dizziness and she braced herself against him. His arm tightened and his other arm slid around her other side, effectively holding her in a firm embrace. She rested her head against his chest and listened to his heartbeat. Then she moved her hands up over his chest to his face and looked into his green eyes for a moment before sliding her fingers into his hair.

"What are you doing?" he asked, his voice a bit raspy now.

"I wanted to see if I was right." She bit her bottom lip. "And I am. Your hair is just as soft as it looks."

"Just what every guy wants to hear."

"We need to go now."

"I totally agree."

But they stood in place in the middle of the room without moving.

Damn, she's so beautiful.

"What did you say?" she asked.

He shook his head. "Nothing. I didn't say anything."

"Weird. I could have sworn you said...well, never mind."

She breathed him in. He wore a familiar men's cologne, but she couldn't think of the name. It was very light, though. Nothing cloying or distracting. She liked it a lot. She liked the warm, sexy way Jacob smelled.

His grip on her grew tighter and his hands slipped down to just below her waist. "Amanda..." he breathed.

She liked how her name sounded when he said it. Like a sigh of contentment. A moan of pleasure.

His gaze was focused on her as she met his eyes again.

She could feel his erection, the hard length of him pressed against her stomach.

You want him to make love to you so much you can barely remain standing, Catherine's words from earlier ran through her mind.

As she realized how true it was, Amanda's breathing came quicker, short gasps of air as Jacob cupped her buttocks and brought her up against him, firmly against that hardness. The sensation managed to make her damp with immediate arousal. It would have stunned her, embarrassed her, if it hadn't felt so damn right.

Unable to control the impulse, she slid her hand down between them and stroked him through the stiff material of his jeans. His erection strained against his zipper and he gasped at her touch.

"What are you—?" he began, but she'd gone up on her tiptoes to crush her mouth against his. The kiss swept whatever he was about to say away. Her mouth opened to him and the feel of her tongue against his coaxed a dark groan from deep in his throat.

For a moment she could have sworn she could read his thoughts. He liked kissing her a lot. He'd waited so long for this to happen.

Her imagination was obviously working overtime. She wasn't a mind reader.

A surge of emotion flowed through her at the feel of his mouth on hers, his hands rubbing her ass and pulling her up closer against his arousal. His muscles tensed as she broke off the kiss and moved her lips down his throat. She moved her hand from the evidence of his desire to pull at his gray T-shirt, lifting it to bare his tanned, muscled chest. He raised his arms, wordlessly, so she could remove the shirt completely. She ran her fingernails down his hot, smooth skin and then drew closer so she could lick a wet stroke of her tongue across his left nipple.

His fingers dug deeply into her sides. *"Amanda."*

The urgency with which he said her name brought her slightly out of her aroused daze. She took a sharp breath, surrounded by the delicious scent of him, still tasting him on her lips and tongue. She wanted more.

A slow realization came over her. This was *Jacob Caine.* She didn't want to spend time with him, didn't want to get assigned as his partner. She'd resisted this with every fiber in her being.

If that was so, then why was she groping him like a drunken woman at last call?

Her mind cleared a little, enough for her to feel a cold sliver of embarrassment. She looked up at him to see there was only desire in his eyes that had darkened significantly.

"It's the clock, isn't it?" she managed, a level of clarity coming into her mind.

"What?"

"It's cursed. That's what Catherine was trying to tell me. It's making us do things we wouldn't normally do. Making us lose control."

He blinked. "Do you really think so?"

"Yes. We need to get out of this room before something really bad happens."

"Okay." His jaw tensed. "Although I have to admit, I don't think I can move at the moment."

She breathed in, immediately distracted as her senses filled again with Jacob. His hot, spicy scent, the taste of him on her lips, her body tingling where he'd touched her, the achingly raspy sound of his voice, the dark look of desire in his eyes. And his body...even with his shirt on she'd known that he was an incredible-looking man. Without it...well, she was at a loss to describe how devastatingly attractive she found him. It sounded like a cliché, but he made her knees weaken.

So that was five senses.

What about the other one?

Her sixth sense was what had gotten them in trouble in the first place.

He released her as if it took a great deal of concentration on his part. "We're not thinking straight. You're right. This must be a spell."

The moment he let go of her she felt bereft. Being close to Jacob, feeling his skin against hers, seemed too necessary and addictive.

She needed him. Catherine had been right. She wanted him to make love to her so badly she could barely think straight.

"We need to go," she said firmly. "Now."

He nodded in agreement, but instead of moving toward the door, he kissed her again, his hands boldly moving down to cup her breasts through her thin sweater a moment before he pulled the cashmere garment off her completely.

"I don't think I can stop this," he said, frowning hard.

Neither could she. Her desire for Jacob at the moment was much too powerful to resist.

"The ghosts said the clock made them lose control." She gasped as he slipped his warm hands under the shoulder straps of her bra to pull them down, baring her breasts. Another gasp when he lowered his mouth and captured her right nipple to suckle on the hard, sensitive pink tip. Desire pooled between her legs, and she had to clutch at his shoulders to stay on her feet.

She felt his hands move to the middle of her back and he unclasped the bra so that it fell to her feet.

She knew she had to stop this, but...well, she didn't really want to. The erotic sensations Jacob gave her were stronger than anything she'd ever felt before. It was as if she'd stuck her finger in a light socket. Only, instead of pain—like the shock wave that came off the clock at midnight—there was nothing but pleasure. She couldn't pull away.

It's not as if she'd never imagined what it would be like to be with Jacob. It was impossible to ignore how attractive he was and how charming he could be—when he wanted to be. Every other woman who crossed his path found him irresistible, why would she be any different?

But this *was* different.

Jacob let out a dark groan that made things low in her body twist with need. She felt his shoulders tense. He dragged himself back from her, though his hands stayed on her breasts as if they were magnetized.

"This is some sort of spell?" he asked.

"Wasn't sure you heard that," she said, finding it hard to concentrate on anything other than his thumbs now circling her very sensitive nipples.

"I was trying to ignore it." His eyes focused on her mouth but instead of making her feel self-conscious, it made her badly want to kiss him again. "You're sure that's what this is? Some kind of magic?"

"What other explanation do we have? It must be a magical trap that's trying to keep us here. Maybe something bad will happen if we can't stop this."

"Then we need to get out of here."

"We do."

"I'm going."

"Okay."

His muscles tightened. "Watch me go."

"I'm watching."

With what seemed to be a monumental effort, he released her and pushed away, averting his gaze from her flushed, half-naked body as he stormed toward the door. The veins stood out on his arms from the effort he put forth, every muscle in his biceps and back tensed. She noticed he had a tattoo on his right shoulder blade—an intricate Celtic knot design in black ink. He grabbed the door handle and turned it. Then he used two hands and rattled the door.

He looked over his shoulder. "It's locked."

She grabbed her discarded sweater from the floor and covered her breasts with it, feeling a fraction more centered and in control with him all the way on the other side of the room. "Break it open, then."

He took a couple of steps back and then kicked the door. It didn't budge. He kicked it again.

No result.

Then he looked at her. "I think we might be trapped in here at the moment."

Instead of being upset at the idea, she felt a warm thrill go through her at the prospect of being trapped in a bedroom with Jacob.

She *so* wasn't thinking straight.

He was breathing faster now, his chest moving in and out as his gaze traveled the length of her. "I need to warn you that I'm not exactly feeling in control of myself here."

"You and me both."

He stalked toward her and she braced herself, expecting him to kiss her again, actually hoping he would. Instead, he breezed past her toward a small table where there was a heavy brass candle holder. He grabbed hold of it.

"What are you doing?" Amanda asked.

"Preventive measures." He handed the object to her.

"For what?"

He stood in front of her looking as serious as she'd ever seen him, his lean, muscled chest going in and out with his labored breathing. "You need to knock me out."

Her eyebrows went up at that. "I need to what?"

"Bash me on the head. Knock me unconscious. Then you'll be safe."

"I'm not safe?"

His jaw was tight. "I can't control myself much longer. I don't want to do anything I'm going to regret."

That statement took her by surprise, and she felt a strange surge of disappointment. "I see. You have enough women in your little black book and you don't want to add my name to the list?"

He just stared at her for a moment. "That's not exactly what I meant."

"What then?"

He exhaled and there was a sheen of perspiration on his forehead now. "I don't want to force myself on you. I feel an overwhelming compulsion to throw you on that bed over there and take you fast and hard. It's close to uncontrollable. If I kiss you again, I won't be able to stop myself. Knock me out while you have the chance."

She tried to process what he was saying. He was trying to be a gentleman? Mr. Lothario I'll-sleep-with-anybody? If she'd been feeling one hundred percent herself, she probably would have rolled her eyes or laughed. But she wasn't.

"Do it," he urged.

She placed the candle holder back on the table.

"Amanda…" His voice held an edge of warning.

"I know," she said. "You don't want to force me to do anything."

"The way I'm feeling—"

"The thing is, I feel that way, too." She dropped the protective covering of her sweater and reached down to take one of his clenched fists in her hand. She brought it slowly to her lips and kissed it. When he unclenched it she slid his index finger into her mouth and then repeated the movement on his middle finger. The look on his face, a visible shattering of that control he'd tried to maintain, was definitely what she was aiming for.

She guided his other hand to her breast. His touch sent an erotic shiver through her body.

She went up on her tiptoes, pressed her mouth against his and pushed away any thoughts that she was doing anything wrong. How could something that felt this right be wrong?

"The clock," he murmured against her lips.

"Later," she replied.

"This isn't real."

"I know." She kissed him again and he finally stopped resisting. She touched his skin, so hot it felt as if it was on fire, burning him up from the inside. "But I need you inside of me now."

He actually growled at that and pulled her against him, flattening her breasts against his chest. The next kiss was harder, deeper, sweeping any remaining thoughts away but one.

This was what happened to Catherine and Nathan, she

thought. *This overwhelming passion.* They'd been unable to resist its pull. And after giving in to that passion they'd been cursed to haunt the house where they'd died.

But then there were no more thoughts, only the sensation of Jacob's hands on her, leaving scorching lines on her skin that made her arch against him.

She undid her jeans so he could help slide them down her thighs. He kneeled in front of her, kissing her sensitive skin and then licked a line over the front of her panties that made her gasp out loud. Jacob stroked his fingers against the damp silk, back and forth, the thin material the only barrier between them.

"You want me," he stated the obvious.

"Yes," she affirmed. "Please."

He stood up and directed her backward toward the bed where she lay down on the soft mattress. He slipped his fingers under the top edge of her panties to slide against her clit. She gripped his wrist, but not to stop him, just to have something to hold on to. Her hips began to move against his intimate touch.

"Do you like this?" he asked.

She nodded, unable to speak at the moment, just feel. And the feel of Jacob touching her as he only had in her personal fantasies was enough to render her speechless.

She wasn't sure what happened to her panties, but they were gone. She was naked with Jacob's hand firmly between her thighs. She looked over at the clock. It had stopped keeping time, staying at midnight exactly.

"You feel so good," Jacob said, and his voice was harsh with need as he leaned over to capture her mouth with his. "You're so wet."

She could still barely speak. "I want you."

His mouth brushed over hers. "I've wanted you from the first moment I saw you."

She heard the soft sound of a zipper. She propped herself up enough to help him pull his jeans down over his thighs. The sight of his hard length made a quiver of anticipation move through her. He pushed her legs wider apart and moved between them.

She brought her hands around to his ass and pulled him closer to her, moving her hips up and down so the tip of his erection slid against her damp flesh, over and over.

"Amanda," he managed. "You're killing me. Please... not yet."

And then, with shaking hands, he was fiddling with something. He'd retrieved a condom from his wallet, his jeans still caught around his knees, and he quickly sheathed himself with it.

"Cursed but responsible," she observed.

"That's me." He managed a small grin that disappeared as soon as it appeared. "Amanda...I can still try to stop this. If you don't want to—"

"I want to. Trust me on that." She brought his mouth down to hers to quiet him, and only a moment later, she felt him push against her, stretching her as he slowly entered her. She wrapped her legs around his waist as he buried himself all the way inside of her.

She knew he was trying to be controlled, but there was no control anymore for them. The stroke of midnight had taken their inhibitions away. Made them desire each other so much that nothing could stop this. She couldn't keep her hands off him even if she wanted to.

You want him to make love to you—

At the time, she'd brushed off the ghost's casual observation, but it was true. She'd wanted Jacob from the moment she first saw him. And despite trying to ignore that desire, it had never left her. She ached for him, for *this*. She'd avoided him at all costs so her crush on him wouldn't distract her.

Hadn't worked very well.

Now she felt him thrust inside of her, his skin against hers, his mouth on the soft, sensitive flesh of her breasts, her throat, her lips. He pulled her up against him then, moving down to grasp her buttocks, fingers digging in to the point of exquisite pain.

"Amanda...Amanda..." He groaned her name over and over. "You're so beautiful. You feel so damn good."

She wasn't sure what she said to him in reply, but she said something. His name in gasps and moans, and then a soft scream left her lips as an orgasm ripped through her, knocking her head backward. His face was between her breasts now and his thrusts became more uneven, faster, her name becoming harder to understand. He kissed her again, his tongue plunging into her mouth.

She concentrated on the incredible friction of him entering her and pulling out. It felt so good, as if this was what had always been missing for her—this overwhelming sensation of being filled completely. His body fitted hers perfectly.

And then, with a last deep, shuddering thrust and a cry torn from his throat he came. The only things moving then were their chests as their breath came back to normal. She wrapped her arms around him, holding him tight against her for several minutes.

Then she stroked his shoulder. "Did you fall asleep?"

"No," was the soft answer.

"Are you going to get off me now?"

His body tensed and he immediately pulled away from her to roll onto his back. He wouldn't meet her gaze.

"I'm sorry," he said.

"For what?"

"For taking advantage of the situation."

She repressed a smile. "Honestly, Jacob. I never knew you had this gentlemanly side to you."

"I normally don't. It must be the spell."

"Right. The spell."

"I should have controlled myself."

"I think that's sort of the point. You can't control yourself. It's impossible."

"Right, but we need to..." He trailed off as he realized that she was caressing his chest now. "What are you doing?"

"Touching you." Her hand drifted down his hard, rippled abdomen and circled his navel.

"I...I can't think properly when you do that."

"Thinking properly is way overrated," she said very seriously. "I think properly all the time and what has it gotten me?" She curled her fingers around his shaft, it was already growing hard again. She leisurely stroked him up and down, bringing forth a low groan from his throat.

"We're going to need another condom," she said. When he didn't answer right away, she leaned over the side of the bed to where his wallet had fallen and retrieved one. She quickly tore open the small packet and rolled it on him before moving to straddle his body. She placed her hands on his chest, feeling wanton and more excited and alive than she'd ever felt in her life.

"Do you want me?"

He looked down at himself. "Isn't it blatantly obvious?"

"That's not an answer. Do you want me?"

"Yes," he hissed. "I want you, Amanda. I've always wanted you."

She lowered herself onto him slowly, an inch at a time, feeling very in control—despite being completely out of control, that is—in this new position. She watched his face as she began to move, his expression of sheer awe and aching need. His gaze moved to their intimate connection and he brought his hand down to stroke his thumb over her clit. The small movement was enough to make her cry out and arch her back as another wave of pleasure crashed over her.

He cupped her breasts as she moved up and down his length, feeling exhilarated, feeling on fire, feeling a passion unlike anything else she'd ever known before. A passion for this man, this difficult man who haunted her as surely as the ghosts haunted this house.

"Jacob," she moaned. "Oh, Jacob, yes. *Please.*"

"Amanda—"

He pulled her down flat against his chest, and then rolled over so he was on top of her again, pressing her down into the mattress, his body thrusting inside of hers deeper and harder and faster until it felt as if they were one person, no beginning, no ending. There was nothing that existed outside of this moment and their bodies moving together as one.

With another cry, he brought her to another earth-shattering orgasm and followed closely behind, his hips straining against hers as he climaxed, murmuring her name into her ear again and again.

She could hear the tick-tock as the clock began keeping

time again. It was over. The spell was broken. They were free to leave the room whenever they wanted.

"I've always loved you," Jacob whispered into her ear just before she fell asleep in his arms.

6

Jacob dragged himself out of the thick fog of unconsciousness.

He must have drunk a whole hell of a lot last night because he had a massive hangover going on. His head felt as if it might split right down the center. Despite that, he actually felt pretty damn good.

That was one hell of a dream.

There was something warm and pleasant in his arms. He was curved around it and it seemed to fit the contours of his body perfectly. Despite the headache from hell, he was quite content to lounge in bed for a while longer. He felt calm, relaxed and strangely happy.

The something warm moved. He pried open an eyelid and glanced next to him. Then both his eyes snapped open as he realized that it was Amanda and he had his arms around her in a tight embrace so her very naked body was pressed firmly up against his.

The realization made him instantly hard. The dream he'd had—the amazing one where he'd made love with Amanda...

It hadn't been a dream at all, had it? He'd had the dream before, in various incarnations, but this was real. She was here.

She let out a contented little sigh as she absently

traced her hands down the line of his spine and back up in a soft caress.

Oh boy.

"Amanda," he whispered. He wasn't sure he could move. The pain in his head now fought with shock and arousal. It was an unusual jumble of emotions to experience all at once.

She nestled in closer to his chest and slowly opened her beautiful blue eyes. A small smile played at her swollen lips and she brought her hand up to his face and brushed her fingers lightly along his jawline.

"Good morning," she said sleepily.

He just stared at her in disbelief.

She blinked, then he watched as realization slowly came over her and her eyes widened little by little until they were dominating her face. Her mouth formed an O as she took in a quick gasp of air.

"What—?" She glanced down at them, covered from the waist down with a thin white sheet, her breasts pressed against his chest, their limbs still intimately entwined. "Oh my God."

There was a sharp knock on the door.

"Why are you still here?" the owner of the house, Sheila Davis, demanded in a loud voice. "You were supposed to call me at the hotel. It's ten o'clock in the morning!"

Amanda grabbed the sheet to pull it higher up before the door swung open. Jacob raised an eyebrow. Guess they weren't magically trapped inside the room anymore.

The spell was definitely over. He exhaled, trying to remain as calm as possible. It wasn't exactly easy.

Sheila took one step into the room, surveyed the two naked people entangled on the bed and her face contorted and reddened with anger.

"What the hell is going on here?" she sputtered. "This is the most unprofessional thing I've ever witnessed in my entire life! I want you out of here *now.*"

She turned around and stomped down the stairs.

Jacob knew he should feel bad that their client had just found them in bed together, but *bad* was one thing he *wasn't* feeling at the moment. Now that he'd had a moment to process what happened, crazy as it might seem, he was pretty damn cheerful. Being with Amanda, something he'd only fantasized about before, had been everything he'd thought it would be. Magical. Mind-blowing.

He craved her again. Would that be really unprofessional? They'd leave in ten minutes.

Or an hour or two. Time would tell.

Other than pulling up the covers, Amanda hadn't moved an inch since she'd woken up. He slid his hand around to the small of her back. He wasn't a cuddler, normally. After sex he usually preferred to be alone if at all possible. But with Amanda, all rules seemed to be thrown out the window.

"She'll get over it," Jacob whispered, brushing his lips against Amanda's ear.

Amanda didn't say anything to that. Instead, she slipped out of his embrace, turned around, and got up from the bed. He had a chance to admire her beautiful body from a distance now instead of up close and personal. He allowed his gaze to casually take in every delicious inch of her as she quickly grabbed her clothes off the floor and just as quickly got dressed, all without saying a word.

She leaned over and grabbed his jeans and threw them at him.

"Where's the fire?" he asked, sitting up so the sheet fell across his lap.

"No fire. Get dressed." The last word was more of a hiss.

He tried to keep the shit-eating grin off his face. "Come on, it's not that bad, is it?"

"Yes, it's that bad." She turned to look at him and her gaze moved over his bare chest to where the sheet draped over the rest of his nakedness. She brought her hands up to her temples and rubbed. Maybe she had a headache like he did.

A magical sex hangover.

Totally worth it, he decided. One hundred percent.

"This shouldn't have happened," she said firmly.

"But it did."

She threw the rest of his clothes at him. "We'll forget about this. Never mention it again."

His smile faltered. "We will?"

She nodded, and he watched as she became more composed and in control with every word she spoke. "Nobody needs to know. Ms. Davis was right. It was totally unprofessional. The clock," she shot it a withering glare as if the inanimate object cared that it was being blamed for the previous night's festivities, "is *cursed*. It made us do...*something*...we normally never would have done in a million years!"

He was getting the strong sense that maybe he was the only one in the room who was okay with what had happened. Amanda obviously wasn't. At all. In fact, she looked ready to throw up or possibly tear her hair out by the roots at the thought that they'd slept together.

Talk about a buzz kill.

"I thought maybe—" he began.

"Jacob, listen to me," she interrupted. "This is bad, okay? We were under a malicious spell. It made us do something that neither of us is proud of. I don't blame you, really I don't. It's best we completely forget it ever happened."

A cold chill slowly filled his veins, effectively dousing the heat of his previous arousal. If there was one thing he was good at in life it was taking a hint from a woman who obviously didn't want him. "Good idea."

"Nobody can *ever* know about this." There was a bit of panic in her voice now. "I can't screw things up. I'm with David and he's wonderful. I'm going to my new job next week and my new life. That's what I want and if anything goes wrong then I don't know what I'm going to do."

"Fine."

"Luckily the...the *spell* seems to be over. I feel totally normal again."

"Me, too."

He got out of bed and tried not to flinch when Amanda purposefully turned her back so she wouldn't have to see his nude body.

It was like having a glass of ice water thrown in his face. She was rejecting him soundly and hell if he would give a damn one way or the other. The raw emotions that had ventured close to the surface retreated back deep inside of him where it was much safer to hang out. The headache remained and he held on to that pain. It was something solid to concentrate on as he got dressed.

He forced a grin onto his face. "It wasn't any big deal for me, anyhow. Just another Friday night. Consider it already forgotten."

He was sure it was only his imagination and wishful thinking that the statement made Amanda wince a little.

DAMMIT. It was supposed to be a simple haunting investigation. That was it. In and out in twenty minutes. Now more than ten hours had gone by—not including drive-time—most of which had been spent unconscious. The rest of it was spent—

Amanda gritted her teeth and stared out of the window as Jacob sped down the highway on their way back to Mystic Ridge, cursing her own lack of self-control. That's what it was all about, wasn't it? When you were a psychic like her it was all about control. Otherwise, she'd have ghosts hanging around her all the time trying to get messages to the living. She couldn't deal with that. It was bad enough dealing with the level of power she used to do her job.

She wouldn't think of last night. She wished the memories would magically fade away, but if anything they were getting stronger as the minutes ticked by. Forget about being haunted by spirits, she was going to be haunted by memories.

Of Jacob.

I'm just one more notch on his bedpost, she thought dryly. She flicked a quick glance at him. He kept his eyes on the road and he'd barely looked at her since they'd gotten in the car. The drive was even more uncomfortable than the ride up. His impossible-to-ignore presence next to her had only been uncomfortably distracting then. Now...well, now was another thing altogether. Now it was torture.

Maybe some of the clock's magic was still at work, because part of her wanted to touch him so badly her hands ached. But she wouldn't. She'd sit calmly next to him with her hands in fists on her lap and will herself to forget how he felt inside her, how good he tasted, how delicious he smelled.

Sure. That would be totally easy.

Luckily, he seemed to be having no problem forgetting.

He'd said as much in the room before they left. Just another Friday night.

After all, the guy wasn't exactly hard up for a date. He could have any woman he wanted.

Then she thought about David, which actually made her feel sick to her stomach. He'd never know about this. It wasn't as if she'd really cheated on him.

She cringed at the thought. Her future with him was still set in stone. It was what she wanted. He'd never understand enchanted clocks and cursed ghosts. He'd simply see it as a breach of trust, especially since he'd suggested they wait to consummate their relationship until after she moved to Manhattan. He was probably the most traditional guy she'd ever gone out with.

She hadn't had sex for a very long time. She hadn't realized how much she'd missed it.

But sex with Jacob wasn't exactly the same as anything she'd ever experienced before. It was...well...*beyond.*

Beyond. Sure, that was a great way to describe something that never should have happened in the first place. Stupid enchanted clocks!

She bit her bottom lip so hard she nearly drew blood.

"So...what?" Jacob said after several more minutes had gone by, and Amanda tried to focus on anything else. "You're not talking to me now?"

"I guess I feel like there's not much to say."

"So, what's the plan?"

She eyed him suspiciously. "What do you mean?"

"Well, I figure the homeowner is not going to go quietly into the good night. She'll be on the phone complaining to Patrick about how she, uh...found us."

Her stomach sank. "You're right."

"So it's not like we can keep it completely between the two of us."

"Obviously Patrick will understand if we tell him what happened."

"And what *was* that again?" He raised an eyebrow. "Just so our stories are straight."

"We were investigating a clock that might have something to do with the curse the spirits are dealing with, and we got...got in the *crossfire* of its magic. And we were temporarily enchanted ourselves and luckily nothing more dangerous occurred."

"*Temporarily enchanted.* That's a good way to put it."

The sarcasm was not lost on her. "I don't know what you want me to say to that."

He shrugged, still keeping his eyes on the road. "I don't know. I was just wondering if any of it could have been remotely real."

She swallowed. "Real? It was a spell."

His eyes flicked to her for a half second. "You seemed pretty into it. In fact, I believe I was the one who wanted to stop, but you basically threw me on the bed and had your way with me."

Her cheeks were on fire. "I'm not having this conversation. It was a spell. A stupid, ridiculous spell and the kind of thing I will happily be getting away from when I quit PARA and move. It meant nothing. Now I would really appreciate if we could change the subject entirely so I can try to forget it."

"*Try?*" His lips twitched.

Her eyes widened slightly. "You think this is funny?"

"Believe me, LaGrange. Funny is one thing I don't think this is."

"That makes two of us."

The edge of amusement in his expression faded and there was a flicker of something else in his eyes. Anger, or...was it frustration?

Before she could figure it out, a flash of pain filled her head so unexpectedly that she yelped. Jacob gasped with pain as well and swerved the car off the road where they came to a stop in a cloud of dust and crunching gravel.

"Damn," he said, holding his head. "What the hell was that?"

"I don't know. It felt like the same thing that happened last night at midnight. The clock..."

"That's exactly what I was thinking."

Oh, no, she thought with a steadily sinking feeling. *It's not over, is it?*

It felt as though a lightning bolt had ripped through the soft tissue between her ears. She closed her eyes and gingerly rubbed her temples.

"What does it mean?" he asked. "We're nowhere near the clock right now."

"No idea."

"Are you okay?"

"Fine. Now I am, anyhow. The pain's gone. You?"

"Just dandy."

She jumped a little and grabbed his hand when he brushed his warm fingertips over her forehead.

"What are you—?" she began.

But she couldn't finish the sentence because he kissed her and in the next moment she was kissing him back as if she didn't have any other choice. It was a compulsion. A compulsion that brought back the events of last night in Technicolor splendor, every detail, every nuance filling her mind, wiping her thoughts away as his tongue slid against hers and her senses were filled with the warm, sexy scent of him. She pulled at his shirt so she could touch his skin and his hands were already up under her sweater cupping her breasts.

The sound of traffic thundering past where they were parked cleared her mind for the briefest of moments, at least until Jacob undid the front of her jeans. His left hand moved down and under her panties to slide between her legs and almost all thought vanished from her mind.

"It's the clock's spell," she gasped, shifting herself closer to his hot touch. It felt way too good to stop him. "We're still enchanted."

His mouth was on hers again and she forgot everything but the pleasure that kissing Jacob brought with it. He felt so good, so right against her. His mouth, his tongue, his hands doing things to her that she couldn't resist. After a brief struggle with her stubborn clothing, her jeans slipped down to the floor and she hazily realized that she was now sitting astride him on the driver's seat.

"Amanda..." he managed. "We're at the side of the road in my car. In public."

"I don't care."

And she didn't.

He let out a dark groan when she undid his zipper and pulled him completely free from his jeans, finding that he was hard and ready for her.

"Condom. Quickly," she urged.

He fumbled for a foil packet. "This is the last one I have on me."

"Hurry...please..."

He sheathed himself, his gaze wild and filled with need

as he met her eyes again. She lifted her hips up to position herself properly then in one smooth stroke, took his full length inside her.

"*Damn—*" Jacob swore through clenched teeth. She traced her fingers along his tight jaw, feeling the rough stubble there. "Amanda, you feel so good. *So good.*"

She leaned forward and cut off any more conversation, such as it was, with an openmouthed kiss.

The steering wheel bit into her back painfully but it didn't make her want to stop. She wasn't sure anything would make her want to stop. She needed this, needed *him* inside her. How could something so wrong feel so completely right?

Her name was a harsh sound from his lips against hers as he began thrusting up into her. He pushed the fabric of her sweater aside and the lacy edge of her bra, to swirl his tongue around her right nipple. The combination of sensations made her arch her back as a shuddering current of pleasure rocked her. It was only a few moments later when he softly cried out her name again, pressing his face between her breasts to muffle the sound of his release.

When the thrusting of his hips ceased she stayed locked against him, her hands pressed to either side of his face, looking into his vivid green eyes. His hands remained low on her hips, half-cupping her buttocks.

"I think we might be in serious trouble," he said gruffly.

The blaring screech of somebody lying on the horn as they zoomed past snapped her out of the daze she'd been in. Something must have changed in her eyes, from passion to clarity, because Jacob's grip tightened.

"No, Amanda, please—"

She got off him and scrambled for her jeans, putting

them on quickly. Unfortunately her underpants wouldn't live to see another day since they were ripped in half. She stuffed the torn patch of silk into her pocket.

And then she went very quiet. She was afraid to speak. She was afraid of what she might say. She might beg him to make love to her again. She hadn't even tried to resist that time. Not even a little bit.

Jacob was right. In the room he'd put up a valiant effort to stop what was going on and she hadn't. She'd wanted it. She'd wanted *him* the way she'd wanted him from the first moment they met.

Did the clock know that?

"Amanda, we need to talk about this."

"No." It came out a little louder than she'd meant it to. She took a deep breath. "We don't need to talk about this. We need to go back home and then we need to never see each other again. Obviously there's something wrong and we need to stay the hell away from each other until we figure out what it is."

She hates me so bad she can't even look at me.

"I don't hate you," she said.

Jacob frowned. "What?"

"I said I don't hate you, even though maybe I should. And I *can* look at you, I just choose not to." She cleared her throat nervously, ignoring the way her body still tingled all over.

"Why do you think I think you hate me?"

"Because you said it."

"No, I didn't."

Is she okay? Maybe all that pain did something bad to her head. Maybe I should take her to the hospital.

"I don't need to go to the hospital," she sighed. "I'm fine, I'm just...a bit disturbed. To say the least."

Jacob was silent for so long that she finally looked at him.

He studied her with a stunned expression. "I didn't say that out loud."

"What are you talking about?"

"The thing about the hospital. That wasn't spoken, but I did think it."

She felt confused. "You must have said it. I heard you."

Can you hear this?

"Yes," she said. "I can."

Jacob's brows drew together. *Oh shit.*

She heard his voice that time also, even though his lips didn't move.

Her eyes widened. "I can hear your thoughts. Why can I hear your thoughts?"

He shook his head. "I have no idea."

"Think something else."

Sorry about the panties. Were they expensive?

She gasped. "I heard that!"

Jacob stared at her for a very long time before a slow grin spread across his face. "That's pretty cool."

"No, it is not cool!" Her mouth was dry. "Last night...right after the flash and the pain I could have sworn I could read your thoughts then just a little. But I ignored it. Now it's much louder and clearer." She put a hand over her mouth to stifle the shock of what she was saying. She could hear what Jacob was thinking. *For real.* "We need to get back to the office before whatever this is gets any worse."

"What else do you think is wrong with us?"

"Other than my reading every thought that flits through your brain thanks to the grandfather clock from hell?"

His mouth quirked. "Don't forget about the fact that you

can't seem to keep your hands off of me. As proven a minute ago. Which, if it wasn't obvious, was fairly *mind-blowing*."

How could he be so blasé about this?

She gritted her teeth. "Drive."

He obliged her without further argument and pulled the car back onto the road. They weren't that far outside Mystic Ridge. Another uncomfortable twenty minutes and they'd be back and ready to deal with this latest disturbing side effect.

She tried to ignore the thoughts moving through Jacob's mind that were mostly memories of her naked. She shot him a dirty look.

"What?" he asked.

"Please stop thinking about me like that. I can't block you out anymore."

She's so cute when she's mad. I can't imagine her boyfriend ever gets her this worked up. Maybe I'm special.

"And stop thinking that, too!" She covered her face with her hands. "Don't bring David into this."

"Consider the subject off-limits."

"Good."

Not long now. Almost back. And then she was going to run as far away from Jacob Caine as she could as fast as her legs could carry her.

JACOB CLEARED his throat ten minutes later. He thought enough time had passed that it might be safe to speak again. "So, you can hear everything in my head?"

"I think so."

That was disturbing. He had some thoughts—hell, he had a *lot* of thoughts—that it would be best that Amanda never listen in on.

If she could really mind-read, thanks to that enchanted

clock, then she would have been able to see that his bravado this morning after her swift dismissal of him had been put on and he was still pissed about being rejected like a piece of garbage.

Shit, he thought. *I can't think that. She'll hear me.*

He glanced at her. She gave no indication of listening in, in fact, she looked as if she wanted to be anywhere but in the car next to him despite what had happened between them just a short time ago. His body was still on fire from the uncontrollable need he felt for her, but his ego was definitely taking a beating.

Maybe this wasn't so bad. Maybe if they spent some time together to break whatever spell this was he could...

What? What was he going to do? Convince her not to move away?

Damn. I'm thinking too much. Have to stop that.

"Yes, please do!" Amanda said. "The sooner the better."

Not good. And he didn't seem to be able to read her mind in return to even the playing field.

He'd thought it was amusing or even interesting for a moment, but this little side effect to their magically induced tryst wasn't even slightly funny anymore. He forced himself not to think about anything except the highway ahead of him as he pressed down on the accelerator.

"This actually brings to mind the conversation we had before we got to the house last night," Jacob said, then gritted his teeth as he thought about it. "Shit. It's like the clock heard us even before we got there."

"What conversation?"

"The one where you told me you know exactly what I'm thinking."

"Did I say that?"

"Yeah, you did."

"A coincidence." But she didn't look convinced.

He gripped the steering wheel a bit tighter. He knew that some spells worked using the energy that the victims already had—passion, anger, fear, love, hate, you name it. If they'd argued about Amanda being able to read his mind and now she could do just that, then maybe it wasn't simply a coincidence. Maybe the clock's spell had latched on to the strong emotions they felt about each other, even before hitting the sheets.

"It was the same conversation where you said I couldn't lie to you," Amanda said, using her unnerving new mind-reading ability to follow along with his thoughts.

"I did say that." He concentrated on the dashed line in the center of the road. If Amanda couldn't lie to him, that would be very interesting. He couldn't remember if he'd asked her any questions that morning. "You don't think that—"

"I don't know."

"How old are you?" he asked with a side glance at her.

"Twenty-seven," she said immediately.

"Is that the truth?" He raised an eyebrow.

She shrugged. "It's the truth, but it's not really that important. I have a few years before I start lying about my age."

He needed another question to test this theory. Something she wouldn't be so open about. "Do you find me attractive?"

"Very," she said and then her eyes widened. "Shit. Maybe we should stop right there."

The previous concern about their bespellment had become amusement again. Wasn't this a fine situation. Amanda LaGrange, unable to lie to him. What possibilities that presented.

He opened his mouth, but Amanda swiftly moved to

clamp her hand down over it. He had to fight to keep the car going in a straight line.

"Be quiet." Her eyes flashed with something that looked a lot like fear. "There's no reason for us to play this game any longer. The clock cursed us last night at midnight and this is another manifestation of that. The ghosts were cursed, too, and you know what happened to them? They were shot to death and now they're stuck in that house until we figure out a way to free them or we exorcise them. We can't mess around with this sort of magic in case it triggers any other side effects."

She is such a party pooper.

"If being responsible is being a party pooper then I guess that's what I am." She glared at him. "If I remove my hand do you promise to behave?"

He nodded.

She removed her hand.

He couldn't resist one more. "Are you really in love with your boyfriend?"

"No," she answered, then groaned at her lightning-fast reply and gave him a look cold enough to flash-freeze the soul of a lesser man. "Why would you even ask me something like that?"

"I was just curious."

She swallowed hard. "Yeah, well, maybe I'm not one hundred percent in love, but I have deep affection for him. He's everything I've ever dreamed of in a man."

He tried not to feel pleased by her answer despite her flimsy attempt to explain it away. He'd known that a woman of passion like Amanda could never be in love with someone like David K. Smith.

What kind of guy said his middle initial when he introduced himself anyway?

7

THERE WAS something seriously wrong with her.

Amanda had been at PARA headquarters for two hours. It was a skeleton crew on Saturdays, but someone was always on call 24/7 in case of emergency. She'd gone directly to her office, even though she really wanted to get in her slate-gray Honda Accord she'd left parked in the back lot and go straight home. She had to input her report. Really, she just wanted to stay busy so she wouldn't have to think. Thinking was bad.

There was an e-mail waiting for her from Patrick.

"I need to speak to you," it read. "See me first thing on Monday."

She cringed, knowing that the angry client had already contacted him about finding her and Jacob sleeping in her bed.

She covered her face with her hands in embarrassment at the thought. It was like an X-rated version of Goldilocks.

She was mortified.

She wanted to forget everything as soon as humanly possible.

It was really a shame that she couldn't think about anything else. And it wasn't only the sex that she was focused on. It was Jacob himself.

She *didn't* feel anything for him, she reminded herself.

Why was that so damned hard to remember?

She'd talk to Patrick on Monday. That gave her the rest of the weekend to process everything and try to make her peace with it. Besides, what was he going to do? Fire her? She'd already resigned. It was just a matter of a few more days before she'd be clearing out her desk and leaving her friends at PARA once and for all.

The thought should have been a relief; instead it just made her feel sad.

In the meantime, she had to find out as much as possible about the house, the ghosts and the clock. She wanted to do what she could to resolve the curse the spirits were under. She'd never been so opposed to an exorcism before.

It should have been simple. Ghosts refused to leave? *Make* them leave.

But it wasn't.

Other than having a strange feeling of compassion for their situation, Amanda had to admit she was more than a bit nervous about herself. Whatever had happened to the ghosts had also happened to her and Jacob. Magic was at work—the magic from that damned enchanted clock— and she needed to make sure it wasn't going to harm them any more than it already had. Or, for that matter, anyone else who might come in contact with it.

She logged on to the PARA database and started hunting for information about the clock, the location of the house and the ghosts themselves.

She found out that a Catherine Myles and her husband had owned the house a hundred years ago. There was no public record of a servant named Nathan that she could find, and the info on Catherine was flimsy at best. Nothing deeper than general facts about her life as a woman married to a rich, controlling businessman in upper New York state. Nothing about an aunt who practiced witchcraft.

After two hours, Amanda felt frustrated with the search. Then again, nothing was ever easy, was it? If she wanted to get the real story she'd have to do a bit more digging. Maybe Patrick would be able to help her. He was great at research. For that matter, so was her friend Vicky.

She sat in her chair and concentrated for a few minutes. At the moment, she felt completely in control of herself. No strange psychic flashes or mind-reading going on. No compulsion to throw anyone down and ravish them shamelessly.

It was very good.

Her cell phone rang and she pulled it out of her purse to answer it.

"Amanda," David said in greeting.

Her eyes widened and she pressed back in her leather swivel chair. "Hi, David. How are you?" Her voice sounded a bit weak.

"Excellent. And you?"

"Wonderful. Really, really great." She tried to put a tone of levity in her words but failed.

He never had to know. It was a spell. She shouldn't feel guilty about it since she'd had no control over what had happened. She would start her new life with David, wonderful David, and everything would be fine.

There was a pause. "You sound upset. Is anything wrong?"

"No, no, I'm fine. It was a late night at work. I was sent on a last-minute assignment."

"You're such a hard worker. What are they going to do without you?" There was a great deal of pride in his voice toward her dedication to her job, which only made her feel worse, if that was possible. "Listen, I wanted to tell you I got a reservation for us at Chez Nuit tonight."

"Okay, great."

"I'll pick you up at seven?"

"Sounds perfect."

And it did. Her wonderful boyfriend was attuned to her wants and needs. He owned his own thriving business. Not that having a boyfriend with money was important to her. She preferred to earn her own spending money instead of having to rely on any man. Her father running out on the family when she was a kid had taught her that at an early age.

Plus, David was very attractive, well-dressed and impeccable in every way.

And they'd never gotten into a single argument. Not one. Although, she figured keeping the true nature of her job at PARA away from him probably helped in this area.

David was, in a word, *perfect*.

Are you really in love with your boyfriend? Jacob's nosy question from earlier poked at her.

No, had been her immediate response, thanks to the clock's spell that seemed to make her compelled to tell him the truth. A very dangerous thing indeed.

However, it *was* true. She didn't love David, but she had faith that she'd *grow* to love him. All of this love-at-first-sight stuff was highly overrated. There was no such thing as love at first sight. Lust at first sight, maybe. And lust faded quickly. A solid friendship, like that she and David had, given enough time to grow and mature into love, would stand the test of time.

She nodded to herself. Time was all she needed. Time away from Mystic Ridge and time away from Jacob Caine.

As far as she was concerned, she never wanted to see him again.

JACOB had decided to never see Amanda the Strange again.

Ever.

It was over.

Completely and utterly over between them. Not that it had ever begun.

He pointed at the shot glass in front of him and the bartender obliged him by filling it up with Jack Daniel's for the...how many was it? He'd lost count. Good job O'Grady's let him keep a tab. He was good for it. He'd never try to get out of any debts he owed for this wonderful, mind-numbing alcohol.

Yes, he was drunk. Being drunk was good. He liked it. He wouldn't like it tomorrow when he would have to deal with the unavoidable hangover, but hell if he gave a damn at the moment.

He eyed his watch—nine o'clock. He still had a whole lot more Saturday night to get through. He was going to keep drinking until he could wipe Amanda's face and body out of his memory forever.

Goodbye, ghost girl.

"Hey!" He motioned for the bartender. "I think I want to make a toast."

The bartender, whose name was Steve, eyed him wearily. "Yeah? What to?"

"To women."

"That's not much of a toast, man."

Jacob held up a finger. "I'm not finished. To women who have screwed me and then screwed me over. May they all rot in hell!"

Steve's lips quirked. "That I'll definitely drink to." He poured himself a shot, clinked glasses with Jacob, and they both sucked down the whisky.

"Again," Jacob pointed at the glass.

"You're not driving tonight, I hope?"

"No way. Left my car at home. The walk'll do me good."

"Fresh air, exercise and all that bullshit."

"That's right."

Steve eyed him. "May I make a casual observation?"

Jacob waved a hand. "Be my guest."

"Normally, when you come in here you're not alone, and I never see you with the same woman twice. Which one are you trying to forget tonight?"

Jacob snorted. "Funny, I've already forgotten."

He wished it was true.

He didn't want to fixate on her. It was sad and pathetic. He didn't do sad and pathetic anymore. He'd left that side of himself in Seattle two years ago when he'd moved here to start a new life.

"Maybe I'll become a monk," Jacob decided.

"That doesn't sound like a very good plan to me."

"I could try it. What's the harm?"

Steve grinned at him. "You know what the best way to get over somebody is?"

"Tell me."

"Get with somebody else. As soon as possible."

Jacob leaned over the bar. "You are a wise, wise man."

"That's why I get paid the big bucks." Steve's grin widened. "And if you don't mind me helping you out a bit, there's a babe over in the corner who's been giving you the eye all evening. I'd put money on her being a sure thing."

Jacob swiveled around on his stool and looked in the direction the bartender had nodded. And sure enough, there was a beautiful blonde staring at him. She wore a short skirt and had fantastic breasts that practically spilled out the top of her tight red top.

"You don't have to thank me," Steve said. "Just send me an invite to the wedding."

Jacob tested his legs by standing up for the first time in an hour and moved toward the blonde without thinking twice. Yes, this was exactly what he needed. He needed to forget Amanda. After all, she already thought he was a womanizer. And that was an accurate enough description, at least until lately. He loved women. Always had.

This woman looked easy to love. Or, maybe she just looked easy.

"Hey, beautiful," he said, then cringed at his words. He could totally do better than that.

Luckily the blonde didn't seem to mind. "Hey. You're Jacob, right?"

"Guilty as charged."

"I've been waiting for the chance to talk to you. I would have gone up to the bar but—" She leaned forward to share some of her cleavage with him. "—I'm *way* too shy."

Sure she was.

"What's your name?" he asked.

"Mandy."

He grimaced. Mandy sounded a lot like Amanda. Too much like it. A thin layer of his pleasant inebriation burned off at the thought.

She patted the seat next to her. "Come sit with me."

He sat. He needed to order more drinks. He couldn't let himself sober up. Not tonight.

"I have to be honest." Mandy's gaze slowly traveled the length of him. "You went out with my sister Emily last

year and she couldn't stop talking about how amazing you
were in bed."

"Oh yeah?" He racked his mind for anything that might
clue him in to who Emily had been. The fact that nothing
came to mind did not make him proud.

"Mm-hmm," Mandy wrapped her hand around his left
knee and began to rub. "I guess I just wanted to find out
for myself."

He nodded stiffly. "Sounds good to me."

"You don't know how good." Her red lips curled into a
sexy smile and she leaned forward to kiss him as her hand
boldly moved up his thigh.

Mandy wasn't bashful, that was for sure.

And he wanted this. A gorgeous blonde with a sexy
little body throwing herself at him? Giving him every indication that she was ready, willing and able even without
having to use his empathic ability to get a read on her true
feelings? That sounded like a very good thing indeed.

At least it did in theory.

She moved away from him and frowned when she realized
that he wasn't kissing her back. "Something wrong?"

He shook his head. "Nothing."

"Don't you find me attractive?"

"You? You're hot. No question."

"Then what's the problem?"

That was an excellent question.

"I don't know," he said.

That was not an excellent answer.

"I want you to take me back to your place," she whispered, and wrapped her arms around him so her large
breasts brushed against his chest. "I'm not normally this

forward, but I really want you, even if it's just for tonight. I'm okay with one-night stands."

Hot blonde. Hot body. Willing to have sex with him with no strings attached.

And he had never been less aroused in his entire life.

Something was seriously wrong with that picture.

He pried her arms away from him. "This isn't going to work."

"Why not?"

"Because..." He grappled for a response. "Because I'm not in a good place tonight. I need to get my thoughts together."

Understanding came over her face. "Is this a girlfriend issue? Because I can be *very* discreet."

The woman was every heterosexual man's wet dream come true.

But Jacob knew that a simple night of sex was not in the cards for him at the moment and it wasn't just because of the alcohol. It was because of the picture seared into his brain.

A picture of Amanda.

A hot line of annoyance burned the rest of his buzz away. *That was Amanda for you,* he thought. *The ultimate buzz kill.*

Then he gripped the side of his chair as another thought occurred to him.

This had to be a part of the curse. The clock was still working its magic nearly twenty-four hours after they'd first come in contact with it. Amanda could read his thoughts and he could make her tell the truth. They were compelled to be together sexually if in close proximity for too long.

And he could not get it up for anybody other than her.

He was in serious trouble.

8

JACOB STAYED at the bar for another half hour before he decided to call it a night. He wasn't sure exactly what tomorrow would bring, but he knew he had to find an answer. He had to find a way to break the curse and the invisible ties that seemed to bind him to Amanda so tightly that he could barely look at another woman.

He emerged into the warm night air and began walking down the sidewalk. His house was less than a mile away and his chosen route there was through the populated area of the small town. Strip malls, restaurants and a multiplex theater.

He didn't want to think about Amanda or what she was up to that night, but he couldn't help it. He absently fished into his pocket and pulled out the digital camera, flicking it on and scrolling past the pictures he'd taken of the grandfather clock. There it was. That's what he was looking for.

It was the shot he'd taken of Amanda in the hall outside the bedroom. She looked over her shoulder at him, her bright-blue eyes burning right into him from her beautiful face. There was a longing in those eyes. A deep, aching need that only he could fill.

Then again, he *had* had a lot to drink tonight. He was probably seeing things that weren't there at all.

"What am I going to do about you?" he asked the picture very seriously.

When the picture didn't respond, he grudgingly shut the camera off and stuffed it back into his pocket. He'd have to download the photos Monday morning at the office. He'd talk to Patrick. Maybe the boss would know what to do, because he sure as hell didn't.

He kept walking, one foot in front of the other, until he passed a restaurant called Chez Nuit. Fancy, expensive French food with cream sauces and hard-to-pronounce names that didn't appeal to him at all. Two people exited the restaurant as he strolled past and his chest tightened as he saw that one was Amanda.

He was about to avert his gaze and keep walking despite the sight of her acting like a lightning bolt straight to his heart and crotch, when she frowned, turned to the left and their eyes met. Hers widened slightly.

Coincidence? he wondered. Or was this chance meeting part of their shared curse? He hadn't been going to take this way home but something had made him turn onto this street that had led him to her. An irresistible compulsion.

She looked incredible in a black dress that fitted her slim but curvy frame perfectly, low-cut enough to give the slightest glimpse of the deep valley between her mouthwa-teringly perfect breasts. She wore her long dark hair loose, draped over her left shoulder. He remembered what that hair felt like running through his fingers; brushing against his face, his lips, his chest. So incredibly soft and it smelled so, so good.

He frowned. Could she read his mind from this far away?

She didn't immediately turn around and run away from him. That was a good start. Pushing aside any fears, he made a beeline directly toward her, his eyes never leaving hers for a second.

"Amanda," he said, but couldn't seem to summon a smile.

She looked nervous. "Jacob. Fancy seeing you here."

"I was spending some quality time over at O'Grady's." He nodded in the direction of the bar.

Damn, she was so beautiful. He couldn't stand it. Why couldn't she be ugly? Maybe that would make this easier. Or, hell, maybe not. He wasn't sure anymore.

She bit her lip and looked down at the ground.

Shit, she heard me, he thought, and then willed his inner voice to shut the hell up before he made any more of a damn fool out of himself.

"Jacob Caine, right?" the man standing next to her said. Jacob had only fuzzily registered that there was anyone else in the vicinity. "We met once before."

Jacob felt the color drain from his face, and he tore his gaze away from Amanda to look at the dude in the suit that probably cost as much as he paid for a month's rent. He was tall, not unattractive, and he held out his hand in greeting. Jacob eyed it warily before shaking it.

"David," he replied, feeling bile rise in his throat. "Good to see you again."

David K. Smith. Mr. Perfect Boyfriend at your service. The man responsible for whisking Amanda away to her so-called normal life in the big city where she could forget about ghosts, curses and Jacob.

"Amanda," Jacob said. "We need to talk about, uh, the job last night."

"You accompanied Amanda on her assignment last night?" David asked in a conversational tone.

Jacob raised an eyebrow. "I did."

"Thank you for taking care of her and bringing her back in one piece."

Jacob gritted his teeth together. He'd taken care of her, all right. "Believe me, it was my pleasure."

He flicked a glance at Amanda to see if she appreciated his choice of words. She looked as if she wanted to shrivel up and disappear. Her gaze was wide and he could practically read her mind, even though that was her talent, not his.

Don't say another word! is what her expression screamed at him.

"You had dinner at Chez Nuit?" Jacob asked.

"Yes," Amanda replied tightly. "It's one of our favorite restaurants."

"We went on our very first date here," David added, and curled an arm around Amanda's waist. "Fond memories."

Jacob smiled tightly. "I'm sure. The food here isn't my style. Did you enjoy your dinner, Amanda?"

"Not really," she said quickly and then her face crumpled and reddened a bit. "I—I mean, of course I did. I loved it." Her eyes moved to David. "It was delicious, really."

He chuckled inwardly. *Can't lie to me at the moment, LaGrange. Remember?*

David looked slightly bemused. "If you say so."

The adoring look on David's face, despite his obvious confusion, was unnerving to say the least. In a way, Jacob wished David was an ogre rather than a nice guy—despite the middle initial—who genuinely liked her. "Listen, Amanda, I need to talk to you."

"Can it wait?" she asked.

"Not for very long."

"Is this work-related?" David asked.

"Of course," Amanda said. "What else would it be?"

What else would it be? Jacob thought drolly. *Other than the fact that we've had sex three times since the clock cursed us? The fact that you can read my mind right now? Wouldn't want your darling boyfriend to know about that, would you? Might put a bit of a crimp in your master plan.*

"Jacob is very dedicated to his job," she added.

Plus the overwhelming need to kiss you right now. I'm not proud. Just putting it out there in case you want to ditch this guy tonight.

She narrowed her eyes at him.

He couldn't help but grin.

Don't worry, beautiful. I'm not going to out you. But we need to talk. I'm serious.

"When is good for you?" he asked out loud.

She crossed her arms. "Tomorrow morning. I'm available to discuss...*business matters*...between ten and ten-thirty."

"Pencil me in."

"I'll do that." She was biting her bottom lip again, obviously a nervous habit, and he found he couldn't stop staring at that lush, sexy mouth of hers.

"Nice to see you again, Jacob," David said.

"Yeah, you, too," Jacob responded half-heartedly, trying to push away any dark thoughts about Amanda's perfect boyfriend. None of this was David's fault. It was nobody's fault, actually.

He'd never understand, would he? Jacob pushed the thought in Amanda's direction.

"No, he wouldn't," she said aloud, then cringed.

David gave her a strange look. "What did you say, Amanda?"

"Nothing." She forced a smile, then glanced at Jacob. "I'll see you tomorrow."

"Count on it."

With a last look at the woman who now haunted his waking hours completely, he turned and forced himself to walk away from her.

AMANDA barely slept that night. She was too busy turning everything over and over in her head and trying to make sense of it all.

But it didn't make any sense.

Even during dinner last night with David she could barely concentrate on the food or wine or conversation. David had been very patient with her, assuming that she'd had a tough, draining assignment the previous night. He didn't grill her about it.

When he'd dropped her off at home after their awkward talk with Jacob outside Chez Nuit, he'd given her a brief kiss on her cheek.

"It'll all be okay," he said. "You're making the right decision. Don't worry."

He thought she was having second thoughts about leaving Mystic Ridge. But she wasn't. If there was one thing she was certain about, it was her upcoming move.

She sat in the middle of her living room surrounded by dozens of packing boxes. Today she was focusing on organizing her massive book collection. Funny how many things one acquired over six years of living in the same place. Boxes and boxes of memories, not including the bags of junk that she planned to donate.

The doorbell rang and she tensed. A glance at the clock told her it was ten minutes to ten. She shook her head. Jacob had never been early a day in his life, but today he was making an exception? Fabulous. Really. Just wonderful.

Last night she'd seen him before she could read his thoughts. She couldn't hear anything until he was within a dozen feet of her. Obviously this mind-reading ability had everything to do with proximity, which confirmed that her recent decision to keep away from him was the easiest way of dealing with this curse. Once she'd left town, the curse would simply cease to be an issue for either of them.

Despite that, she pushed away the annoying shiver of anticipation she got at the thought of seeing him again and rose to her feet. This would be simple. She'd tell him her plan to discuss matters with Patrick at the office tomorrow, get his feedback, but otherwise pretend that nothing had happened. As far as she was concerned, nothing *had* happened.

Do you even lie to yourself? her inner voice scolded.

The fact that she could barely touch David last night was an indication of how self-delusional she was being. Her awkwardness with him wasn't only because of the guilt she felt at betraying his trust. It had been a whole day since she'd last had sex with Jacob, but it felt as if his body had branded her. When she closed her eyes it was his face she saw, not David's. That was disturbing on too many levels to count.

Not because of how Jacob had made her feel when they'd made love, but because she knew it wasn't real.

She knew beyond a shadow of a doubt that it was fake because it was too big, this feeling inside her; she'd never felt this kind of overpowering need before in her entire life.

If she thought it was real, if she let herself explore the sensations and emotions he'd effortlessly coaxed from her...then she'd be in more trouble than she already was. Because if she was truthful with herself, she'd liked it. She'd liked *him*. Everything about him and everything they'd experienced together. She knew she could easily fall head-over-heels in love with Jacob Caine if she let herself.

And that wasn't going to happen. Not a chance.

She reminded herself of this sternly as she opened the door, fixing a frozen smile on her face, and was surprised at who stood on the other side. It was a well-dressed, dark-haired woman in her midfifties who was extremely familiar despite Amanda not having seen her for a few months.

"Mom?" she squeaked. "What are you doing here?"

"I came to see if the rumors I've heard were true." Her mother's gaze moved past her daughter and into the small house. "And they are. You're finally moving away from this dreary little town?"

"I...I am. Yes."

Madeleine stood there for a moment tapping her right foot. "Are you going to invite me in?"

Amanda snapped out of her daze and waved an arm. "Of course. Please, come in. I have coffee made. Would you like a cup?"

"I'm drinking green tea now. Do you have any of that?"

"Sorry, no." She awkwardly hugged her mother, trying to get over her surprise at this impromptu visit. "Come in, have a seat."

"I can't stay long."

"I understand. But it's so wonderful that you dropped by."

Her mother's new husband was a banker. She'd only seen Madeleine twice since the wedding last year, but both times she'd been wearing only the best, most expensive fashions, and her hair had always been perfectly in place. This was a far cry from the woman Amanda remembered from her childhood, who'd had to take on two jobs after Amanda's father had left them without any savings.

She pushed the painful memory away.

"Where are you moving?" her mother asked, glancing at the boxes.

It said quite a lot about their relationship that she'd neglected to mention her upcoming move to her mother. She was sure she would have gotten to it, given enough time. She already had those change-of-address notices filled out.

"New York City," she said. "Manhattan."

Her mother raised an eyebrow. "Is this because of a man?"

"No. Not entirely. I thought it was time for me to start new somewhere. I'm going into the advertising business."

"Really?" Her mother seemed surprised by this. "I thought you were perfectly happy working for that strange little company here. After all, it's been how many years now? Four?"

"Six, actually. I guess I needed a change."

"So you won't be requiring your unique...*skill set*...at the new job?"

Her mother had never referred to her psychic abilities except in the most vague and disapproving terms possible. "That's right."

"Very interesting. And you said 'not entirely' because of a man, but there is someone involved?"

"Yes. His name is David and I'm moving to be with him."

"Is he..." Her mother pursed her lips. *"Different?"*

"If you're asking if he's psychic, no he isn't. David is the most normal man I think I've ever met. I'm sure you'd love him."

This brought the first smile she'd seen on her mother's face in as long as she could remember. "This is wonderful, Amanda. Finally, after all this time you've seen the light. You see that your current lifestyle would not bring

NO POSTAGE
NECESSARY
IF MAILED
IN THE
UNITED STATES

BUSINESS REPLY MAIL

FIRST-CLASS MAIL   PERMIT NO. 717   BUFFALO, NY

POSTAGE WILL BE PAID BY ADDRESSEE

THE READER SERVICE
PO BOX 1867
BUFFALO NY 14240-9952

Play the Lucky Hearts Game

and get...

2 FREE BOOKS and 2 FREE Mystery GIFTS... YOURS to KEEP!

yes! I have scratched off the gold card. Please send me my **2 FREE BOOKS** and **2 FREE Mystery GIFTS** (gifts are worth about $10). I understand that I am under no obligation to purchase any books as explained on the back of this card.

Scratch Here!
Then look below to see what your cards get you... 2 Free Books & 2 Free Mystery Gifts!

We want to make sure we offer you the best service suited to your needs. Please answer the following question:
About how many NEW paperback fiction books have you purchased in the past 3 months?
❏ 0-2 ❏ 3-6 ❏ 7 or more

351 HDL EZK9   151 HDL EZLL

FIRST NAME   LAST NAME

ADDRESS

APT.   CITY

STATE/PROV.   ZIP/POSTAL CODE

Visit us online at www.ReaderService.com

Twenty-one gets you
2 FREE BOOKS and
2 FREE MYSTERY GIFTS!

Twenty gets you
2 FREE BOOKS!

Nineteen gets you
1 FREE BOOK!

TRY AGAIN!

▼ DETACH AND MAIL CARD TODAY! ▼

(H-B-09/09)

© 2009 HARLEQUIN ENTERPRISES LIMITED. Printed in the U.S.A.
® and ™ are trademarks owned and used by the trademark owner and/or its licensee.

you the future you so deserve. All I've ever wanted for you was the chance to be normal and happy."

Normal and happy. A mutually exclusive pairing?

The doorbell rang again and Amanda's stomach sank. She considered ignoring it, but that wasn't a very good solution. Jacob struck her as a persistent man when it came to getting what he wanted.

"Just a moment," she told her mother and went to the door. The sight of Jacob swept her breath away for a moment. Today he wore a dark-green button-down shirt that made his green eyes more noticeable, and dark jeans. Despite everything, she felt herself weaken a bit as the desire she desperately tried to repress swirled inside of her.

He actually gave her a half smile. "Good morning."

"This isn't a good time."

The smile faded. "We had an appointment."

"I know. But, my...my mother is here. I didn't expect her."

"Who is it, Amanda?" her mother called from the living room.

Jacob raised a dark eyebrow. "Your mother? I would love to meet her."

She almost smiled at how inappropriate that idea was. "Not a good idea."

"I disagree."

"Why am I not surprised?"

He leveled his gaze with hers. "You said we could talk. We need to talk. I don't want to put this off any longer. Please, let me come in."

Being this close to him was dangerous, but she finally stepped aside to let him into her house. As he brushed past her, the briefest contact brought with it a dangerous storm warning for her growing inner hurricane.

THE WOMAN looked so much like an older version of Amanda he would have known it was her mother without being told. After all, he'd memorized every nuance of her daughter's face. He couldn't erase it from his mind if he wanted to.

She shared Amanda's beautiful smile, as well. "You must be David," she said. "Amanda, he is very handsome."

Amanda moved toward her mother's side, carefully avoiding Jacob's eyes. "No, this isn't David, actually. This is...uh...Jacob Caine. He's a coworker of mine. Jacob, this is my mother, Madeleine Harper."

The smile faded from Madeleine's face and was replaced with an expression of disapproval. "I see. A coworker, you say?"

Amanda nodded and studied the floor.

"Great to meet you," Jacob said. "And thanks for calling me handsome."

Amanda's lips quirked at that as she repressed a smile.

So this was the woman who didn't approve of her daughter and had made her feel abnormal because of her abilities, huh? He could barely believe what Amanda had told him last night, that her father had abandoned their family because he couldn't deal with having a psychically gifted daughter.

The thought made his blood boil. Who would turn their back on their family for a stupid reason like that? No wonder Amanda had major hang-ups about what she could do. She'd never been properly nurtured. Nobody had told her while growing up that there was absolutely nothing wrong or abnormal about her.

Instead she'd grown up feeling like a freak of nature for being psychic, and that was so deeply embedded in her that she couldn't see any differently now that she was an adult.

She couldn't see how wonderful and amazing she was. Well, he could see it. He could see it only too clearly.

Amanda's forehead was furrowed in a frown and she raised her gaze to his.

Shit, she heard me, he thought. *Why do I have to think so much?*

Madeleine was studying them a bit too intently. "Where is David right now, dear?"

Amanda's shoulders stiffened. "On his way back to his office in New York."

"He works on Sundays?"

"He's very dedicated to his job. He owns the company. He'll be back for my going-away party on Tuesday night and then he'll stay to help me move out on Wednesday."

Madeleine looked satisfied with that answer. "He sounds like a wonderful man."

Yeah, Jacob thought. *Wonderfully, boringly normal. You'd definitely approve of the wonderfully, boringly normal life he plans to give your daughter.*

That earned him a sharp glare from Amanda, but he ignored it. It amused him a little that he could still push her buttons without even saying a word out loud.

"You said you came here for a meeting?" Madeleine directed the question at Jacob.

"I did."

"I'm curious about what kind of a meeting my daughter had planned for a Sunday morning just as her boyfriend has left town."

Jacob repressed a smile. "It is unusual timing, isn't it?"

Madeleine wasn't amused. "I know I'm not a large part of my daughter's life anymore, but I am fully invested in her happiness. And I'm also a quick study.

From what I gather, she's found that happiness with David. Enough so that she's leaving this horrid little town to be with him."

"She hasn't left yet," Jacob said. "Not for three more days."

"Jacob and I have a case to discuss, that's all," Amanda interjected.

"Haven't you quit your job?"

"Yes, but—"

"Honestly," Madeleine waved her hand. "If it were me, I'd want to get as far away from this insanity the moment I was given the opportunity."

"Would you?" Jacob said dryly.

She fixed him with a steady gaze. "I would."

He didn't have to know Amanda's mother very long to get a good sense of her. The woman had lived a hard life. She was a survivor. She had a very fixed idea of what was right and wrong and it would take a lot to make her deviate from that opinion. He didn't think she was a bad woman, but there was a hardness to her, an edge, that he'd seen glimpses of in Amanda herself. This was Amanda in twenty-five years. This was Amanda if she repressed her abilities because she didn't accept herself. No passion, no spark, just somebody who thought they knew best.

"I think you should leave," Amanda said aloud. She'd listened in on his thoughts and hadn't liked what she'd heard.

"Do you really want me to leave?" he asked, wanting to coax the truth out of her.

"Yes," she responded.

Sometimes the truth hurt.

"It was a pleasure meeting you," he lied and held a hand out to Madeleine, who shook it since it was the polite thing to do.

"Likewise," she said.

He squeezed her hand and opened up his mind to hers—his psychic ability that helped him get a read on people. It was the reason he'd been recruited to work for PARA, after all. His empathic ability was similar to reading someone's mind, but not exactly. After all, one could lie with their thoughts, but they couldn't lie with their subconscious. And that's what he tapped into.

He allowed the images to move through his mind, hoping that Amanda could also see them as clearly as he could.

Amanda's mother had a very flimsy hold on her pleasant-faced control. The immediate hate she felt toward Jacob was evident in her subconscious. She saw him as part of the problem; part of what she loathed, which was anything she didn't understand. She didn't like psychics. Her strong religious beliefs didn't mesh with accepting anything supernatural. To her, a psychic of any kind represented all that was unnatural and evil.

"Will you please let go of my hand?" she asked evenly.

"In a moment," Jacob said. "I have a question for you first, if you don't mind."

Her smile held, although there was no warmth in her cool blue eyes. "What is it?"

"Did your husband really leave you because of Amanda? Because he feared her clairvoyancy? Did he think she made that ghost push him down the stairs? Or did he leave for an entirely different reason?"

A flash of anger went through her gaze. "Our personal lives are none of your business."

"No, you're right. But I'm curious. I'm getting the sense that you have held a lot back from Amanda. Do you know what it's done to her? Do you have any idea how much your lack of approval has shaped the way she leads her life and sees the world around her?"

"I don't know what you're talking about."

But she did. He could feel it under the surface. Repressed memories, ignored for years. Pain and heartbreak covered up with lies until the lies became larger and more damaging than the truth.

But at the heart of it, he could see a mother doing what she could, in her own way, to protect her daughter. A daughter of whom she didn't approve of. A daughter she wished was what she perceived as "normal."

And he knew then that Madeleine's husband hadn't left her because of Amanda's psychic abilities. He'd left because he was an asshole. The Amanda excuse had seemed convenient at the time, that was all.

"Jacob, stop this." Amanda's arms were crossed in front of her.

He finally let go of her mother's hand. She stared daggers at him, but underneath that angry expression, he could see a sliver of uncertainty.

"She deserved better," he hissed at the woman. "And you know it."

"Jacob—" Amanda said sharply. "I'll see you tomorrow at the office and we'll figure this out, okay? I want you to go now. Please."

He stared at her for a long moment, and then tore his gaze away. "Fine."

He left, slamming the door to Amanda's house behind him. The house she was packing up to leave—along with her present life and him—behind.

He just wished it didn't feel so damned bad.

9

AMANDA was quiet for a very long time after Jacob left. Her first impulse was to run after him, to apologize for being so harsh, but she forced herself to remain standing in place.

"He was very unpleasant," her mother said. "I have no idea why you'd want to spend any time at all with someone like him."

She didn't reply to that. She was too busy watching the black Mustang peel out of her driveway. He was too far away for her to hear his thoughts anymore. The last thing she'd heard was something about her leaving him. The thought seemed to be edged with pain.

He'd shared other thoughts with her, as well. Thoughts about her mother that he'd gleaned from her subconscious. Thoughts that made her wonder what the truth really was.

"I really must be going." Her mother cleared her throat after another few moments passed in silence. "Charles will be expecting me back soon."

Her husband, Charles. The perfect rich guy who bought her nice things and made her life very comfortable after a lifetime of struggle.

"Is it true?" Amanda asked quietly.

Her mother frowned. "Is what true, dear?"

"Dad," she began. "When he left—"

"Please, let's not talk about that."

"We never have talked about that. You always change the subject."

"It was an unpleasant time of our lives that I have no intention of reliving."

"Did he leave us because he didn't want to be around a daughter who had the ability to attract ghosts?"

Madeleine pursed her lips. "That was part of it, of course."

"Part of it?" Amanda repeated, and she swallowed past the thick lump in her throat. "I thought...I've always thought that was the main reason he left us."

"This is precisely why I don't like to discuss the past. It's upsetting. Both to you and to me."

"Jacob said—"

"Jacob?" her mother cut her off. "I don't know who this Jacob person really is, but don't let yourself be influenced by him. He's trying to manipulate you. Trying to get you to stay in this town. It's obvious to me that he's in love with you, and he won't accept that you've found happiness with someone else."

This stunned her. "Jacob isn't in love with me."

"All I know, honey, is that love is not the answer. Love will only lead you into misery. I loved your father and he left me with nothing."

"You had me."

Her mother blinked hard at that and pressed her lips together. She reached forward and squeezed Amanda's shoulder. "I think you will see this situation much more clearly when you leave here, get away from Jacob, and all of this craziness. I think you've chosen correctly. I don't know David, but I get the sense that he is the right man for you and will make you very happy. I want you to be happy, honey, I really do."

"I know." She hugged her mother briefly before saying a last goodbye and promising to be in touch. Then Madeleine Harper got in her Mercedes and drove away.

SHE DIDN'T HEAR from Jacob again that day and she busied herself with packing up everything that wasn't nailed down. She'd miss her little house and her neighbors. It was a nice area, and in the fall the oak tree out front turned a beautiful color.

She picked up the phone at nearly eleven o'clock that night and was about to dial Jacob's number that she had found in the company directory, but she stopped herself. Whatever she had to say to him, and she wasn't exactly sure what that might be, could be said at the office tomorrow.

The fact that her mother thought that he was in love with her made her want to laugh. What a ridiculous notion.

She let out a shuddery breath and decided to go to bed. By eleven-thirty her head was on her pillow and she willed the storm of thoughts competing for mental space to go away. Finally she drifted off.

But, of course, she dreamed about him.

She was lying on a lounge next to a swimming pool at an upscale tropical resort and soaking up the warm sunshine. She lowered her sunglasses as Jacob walked past and spotted her. He wore baggy blue swim trunks and no shirt. His muscled chest was bronzed and absolutely perfect.

"Amanda LaGrange," he said. "Fancy seeing you here."

There were only the two of them in the pool area. Even the swim-up bar was unoccupied.

"I can't escape you, can I?" she said, feeling amused by

the dream and how incredibly irresistible and sexy her subconscious made Jacob look.

It actually wasn't much different from how he looked in her waking life, although he wore fewer clothes in the dream.

His gaze swept over her barely there black bikini. "You look so good."

"Thank you."

He grinned and glanced around their surroundings. "I can have you all to myself here. Nobody to interrupt us."

"Do you want me all to yourself?" she asked.

"You know I do. But this isn't real."

She swung her legs over the side of the lounge chair and then got up to close the distance between them. She ran her hand down his arm. "Feels pretty real to me."

"It does, doesn't it?" His Adam's apple shifted as he swallowed. "You are so beautiful. I want you so much, Amanda, I can barely keep my hands to myself right now."

The statement thrilled her. She desperately hoped nothing would wake her up for a while as she explored all the delicious possibilities this situation presented.

She reached around to the back of her bikini top and undid it, then shrugged it off. It fell to the ground. Jacob's appreciative gaze slid down the front of her.

She turned around to press her backside against him, feeling his erection against it, and brought his hands up to her breasts. "Then don't keep your hands to yourself. I want you to touch me."

He didn't resist. He rubbed his thumbs over her tight nipples which shot a hot line of desire straight to her groin.

"This is very good," he said as one hand drifted down her belly to slide into her bikini bottoms. He stroked his fingers against her sex. Her breath came quickly now but she didn't want him to get the upper hand, so to speak, quite so quickly.

She turned around and undid the loose tie at the front of his trunks and slid the elastic down over his hips to free his erection. She took him in her hand. Licking a hot wet line down the center of his chest and over his washboard abs, she settled down onto her knees in front of him and took him in her mouth.

Jacob swore loudly as she worked his length with her hand and mouth, skimming her tongue along his hard, thick shaft.

She felt so free. This was what she wanted, to have him like putty in her hands. To have him moan her name over and over. When they'd made love when she was awake it had been a blur, a wonderful orgasmic blur, but she hadn't felt in control of herself. Here, she was. It was her dream and she could do anything she wanted.

She wanted it to be real. She wanted him here with her with the sun on their bodies as they made love with no restraint or second-guessing.

"Amanda," Jacob moaned her name. "Too good. It feels too good. I wish this wasn't a dream. I want you so much."

Yes, just a dream.

She licked and kissed her way back up his body while her hand still stroked his length. She concentrated on his throat, the underside of his stubbled chin, his lips that parted for her, his tongue sweeping against hers. She was so ready for him. She wanted him inside her so badly that she ached.

"My favorite dream ever," she said out loud.

"Definitely," he agreed.

He skimmed her bikini bottoms down her legs and then leaned over to kiss her flat stomach, parting her with his fingers so he could slide his tongue against her. She gasped and arched her back, fisting a hand into his black hair as he pleasured her with his mouth. She'd never had a dream that felt so real before.

Kissing a hot trail back to her mouth, he got to his feet and lifted her into his strong arms, a dark, frenzied look now on his face. "I need you."

She just nodded. Yes. She needed him, too. More than he'd ever know.

He carried her back to her lounge chair, laying her gently down on her back. She looked up at him.

"This can't be your favorite dream," he said. "Because it's *my* favorite dream."

She groaned as he parted her legs and rubbed the tip of his shaft against her entrance. He was teasing her when all she wanted was to be filled.

"Don't need protection in my dream," he said with a crooked grin.

"*My* dream," she said.

"*Mine,*" he corrected. "But let's not argue. That's what we do when we're awake."

She wanted him inside of her so badly that she couldn't think straight, but despite the incredible pleasure she felt, she frowned. "You're saying this is *your* dream?"

He nodded, and leaned forward to brush his mouth against hers. "I earned it after that scene at your house today. Your mother is fairly horrible. I don't think she'll ever accept me as her son-in-law."

"This isn't your dream. It's *my* dream."

He smiled. "Afraid not. I think I know when I'm dreaming. Now if you don't mind, I'm trying to concentrate here. Wouldn't want to wake up yet. You feel way too good."

"This is my dream," she said again. "It's a good one, amazing in fact, but it's still my dream."

"Possession is nine-tenths of the law," he whispered against her lips.

"What if...what if we're both dreaming?" she asked, sliding her hands up to his broad shoulders. "What if this is just another manifestation of the curse?"

He frowned. "That's impossible."

"Is it?"

He leaned back to look at her and there was something in his green eyes that made her believe he didn't think it was so impossible. That he was seeing that she wasn't simply a naked figment of his imagination.

"I don't want to wake up," he said.

"Then kiss me," she suggested, and he didn't need to be told twice. He kissed her hard and deep and she tried desperately to hold on to the feeling of his body against hers, almost inside her—so close—touching, tasting the smooth, hot skin against hers. And in the next moment, all of those sensations vanished and there was no pool, no resort and no Jacob.

As she woke, she opened her eyes to find that she was staring at the ceiling, her body covered in perspiration, her bedsheet twisted around her. A dark, unfulfilled need gnawed away inside of her.

Her phone rang. She reached over to grab it and pressed it up against her ear.

"Yeah," she managed.

"So was it?" Jacob asked quietly. "Or wasn't it?"

She swallowed hard and licked her dry lips. "It was."

There was a pause for so long that she thought he might have hung up on her. And then, "We have to find a way to break this curse."

"I agree."

"We'll fix this. I promise."

"Okay."

"Goodnight, Amanda."

"Goodnight, Jacob."

She clicked the phone off, her body still aching for his touch.

She stared at the ceiling knowing there was no chance she was going to be able to get back to sleep again that night.

"I SEE," Patrick said, leaning back in his wheelchair and tenting his fingers. "Yes, that is a problem, isn't it?"

He glanced at his two favorite employees, who both looked beside themselves with stress over this situation, and he tried desperately not to laugh.

It wasn't funny.

Well, maybe a little bit.

When he'd sent them out on the assignment together the other night he'd had no idea it would get so out of control. He'd woken up to the shrew of a client screaming at him from the other end of the phone on Saturday morning. So much for giving out his cell phone number to customers. He'd needed the weekend to relax before he dealt with the repercussions. After all, this was kind of his fault.

He hadn't anticipated an enchanted clock, though. He'd just thought that spending some time together would make these two realize they didn't hate each other and maybe there was something more between them that they'd want to explore.

So much for playing matchmaker.

"What do you suggest we do about this?" Amanda asked tightly.

It was so obvious that they'd had sex. They had yet to admit that to him, but he was no dummy. His psychic skills leaned toward Jacob's—an empathic ability—although Patrick didn't have to touch somebody to see the truth of what they felt. He just had to be in the same room with them.

At least somebody was getting some. He hadn't had sex since before his accident. *Well* before. The doctors promised that his equipment would be back in working order eventually. But his sorry sex life didn't have much to do with the current problem at hand.

"So, there's a witch involved," he said. "The one who enchanted the clock in the first place."

Jacob nodded and darted a sideways glance at Amanda. His arms were crossed tightly over his chest. "The former owner of the house, Carolyn—"

"*Catherine* Myles," Amanda corrected. Jacob glared at her. "It was her aunt. And it was a wedding gift a hundred or so years ago. Her aunt apparently didn't approve of her choice of a husband. I'm guessing that the aunt sensed he had murderous tendencies and she was trying to protect Catherine. But giving her a wedding gift like the grandfather clock doesn't make any sense, considering what it does."

"The clock's magic caused Catherine and her servant Nathan to begin a physical relationship," Patrick said. This was the second time they had gone through this part of the story.

"That's right," Amanda said. "And the false feelings that they developed made it look as if they were in love and her husband shot them both."

"You think they were false feelings?" Jacob asked. "The way you described them to me made me think they really were in love. You were all about their star-crossed romantic lovefest when we were at the house."

Amanda was quiet for a moment. "I did get the feeling that Nathan was in love with Catherine—he said as much. But the more I think about it the more I'm not so sure she felt the same in return. Maybe it was only lust for her."

"Unfortunately I didn't see or speak to the ghosts," Jacob said. "Not my talent."

"And when the clock struck midnight, what exactly happened?" Patrick asked carefully.

"Well," Amanda said as she and Jacob exchanged a glance. "I can only compare it to a feeling of, uh...a sense of, um...how do I put this?"

"She tore my clothes off and had her way with me," Jacob finished.

Amanda gasped. "That's not how it was."

"No?" He raised his eyebrows. "Then how was it?"

She gritted her teeth and looked at Patrick. "We were compelled to do things we normally wouldn't have done. And I'm very sorry that the client had to witness us in a very...um...unprofessional position."

"Lots of unprofessional positions," Jacob added. "My favorite was the one where you were on top of—"

"*Shut up!*" Amanda's face was so red that she looked ready to pop.

Do not laugh, Patrick commanded himself. *The woman might actually kill somebody.*

"Come on," Jacob persisted. "It was the best sex of your life, right?"

"Yes, it was," she replied immediately, and then her face darkened a shade. "Please don't do that anymore!"

Right, Jacob was able to get her to tell the truth. And in turn, she could read his mind. This was seriously messed up.

"I am not a relationship counselor," Patrick said after a moment. "So your sex lives are none of my business. But enchanted objects and spirits who refuse to go onto the next world are. I'm going to look over your paperwork and photos and decide what to do next. I'm thinking an exorcism is definitely in order. As far as the clock, perhaps if it is dismantled and burned with some cleansing oil, that might take care of breaking your curse."

Neither of them looked satisfied with that answer. Despite Jacob's flippant manner, Patrick could see the tension in his expression.

"Fine," Amanda said stiffly. "If you think that's the best course of action, then that's what we'll do. I'll wait for the exorcism orders. However, I'd like to do a bit more research first, if that's okay."

"Be my guest," Patrick said. "One way or the other, we'll work this out. After all, it doesn't seem to be a dangerous curse, just an inconvenient one, right?"

He didn't receive any reply to that statement.

"If you'll excuse me," Amanda said. "I have to get back to work."

She left the office and Jacob watched her leave with a wistful look in his eyes. He made a move to follow her, but Patrick stopped him.

"Close the door, Jacob," he said. "I'd like to speak with you privately."

Jacob's shoulders tensed, but he did what the boss told him to and turned around to face Patrick. "Yeah?"

"Is it just the curse or are you really in love with her?"

Jacob's eyes bugged. "What?"

"Did I stutter?"

"No...it's just that...I'm not..." He blinked hard, color slowly draining from his face. "I'm not in love with her. Lust, sure. But...but love?"

"Right. So you're still in denial about it, are you?"

"I'm not in denial. I'm..." Jacob swallowed. "I...I just don't know what's real anymore. She's the most stubborn and frustrating woman I've ever met, but all I want is to be with her. It's driving me insane, actually."

"It'll get better."

Jacob laughed at that. "Promise?"

"Actually, no. I was just trying to be helpful."

"Great."

"Maybe she'll change her mind and stay in Mystic Ridge."

Jacob shook his head. "She won't. She's leaving and nothing I can say will make a damn bit of difference. She's focused on her new, normal life with her boyfriend."

"Nothing you can say will make a difference? Have you said *anything?*"

"Some. I told her she was making a mistake by turning her back on her talents."

"Did you tell her you're in love with her?"

Jacob blanched again. "I thought I already told you—"

"That you're not. Lust only, thanks to the spell. I almost forgot. Do you want my unsolicited advice?" Patrick didn't wait for a reply. "If you discover it isn't just lust, tell her how you feel. Tell her you don't think it's just the curse that makes you feel that way. Put the ball in her court. At least then, if she still chooses to leave, she'll be making an informed decision."

Jacob was quiet for a long moment. "I don't think it's just lust."

The corner of Patrick's mouth twitched with amusement. "No shit."

"But what if we break the curse and I stop feeling this way about her?"

"Do you think you will?"

Another pause. "No."

"Then go talk to her. Her going-away party's tomorrow night. It's not like you have a lot of time to make this work."

"I'm going to look like a damn fool."

"That's very possible." Patrick shrugged.

"I think I hate you."

Patrick smirked at him. "You're fired."

Jacob grinned and let out a long shaky sigh. "You know, I had a chance to hook up with a random babe last night and I couldn't do it. I couldn't get excited. I thought for a moment that it was another side effect of the curse, but now I'm thinking that I'm just not attracted to anyone else."

"Maybe you're in more trouble than I originally thought."

"Comforting. Thanks." He looked over his shoulder at the closed door. "Can I go now?"

"Be my guest."

Jacob moved toward the door and opened it up.

"One more thing, Jacob," Patrick said. Jacob turned to look at him. "I hope it all works out."

"Me, too." With that, Jacob left his office.

Patrick wished he had the ability to see into the future. It would be very handy right now.

10

AMANDA could barely concentrate on the computer screen in front of her. She was finding nothing helpful in her research and it was driving her crazy. She knew not everything under the sun was documented and neatly organized, but it would be nice if it was.

There was a knock at her door and she tensed, thinking it was Jacob. After their sexy shared dream last night, it was safer if she didn't see him alone. She was embarrassed at how easily she'd accepted the opportunity to do things to and with Jacob that she resisted in her waking hours. He'd seen how much she wanted him, despite her many protests. And he'd just made her admit that sex with him had been the best of her life.

Well, it *had* been. But that didn't make it okay.

Destroying the clock had been a solution she'd already thought of but she'd hoped that Patrick, with his ultimate knowledge of the supernatural world, would have a better and quicker solution.

Her original decision to simply ignore the curse until she moved away wasn't feasible anymore. If they could find each other in their dreams, then no distance would make a difference. She felt bound to Jacob, body and soul, at the moment, unable to think about anyone else or even concentrate on the last two days of her job at PARA.

She rubbed her temples. "Come in," she said when the knocking persisted despite her best attempts to ignore it.

The door opened and in walked her best friend Vicky, who held two cups of coffee in her hands, one of which she gave to Amanda. Vicky was a few inches taller than Amanda, very attractive, with medium-length dark-blond hair, and she liked to dress in low-cut tops and short skirts. Usually her clothes were some shade of purple. Today was no exception. She was also clairvoyant, although it took her a little bit more effort to see ghosts than it did Amanda.

"Good morning," she said with a smile.

Amanda smiled back and took a sip of the strong brew. "'Morning."

"You forgot the *good*."

"No, I didn't."

Vicky laughed at that. "How's it going?"

"Fine," Amanda lied.

Vicky studied her for a moment. "Well?"

"Well what?"

"Are you going to share or do I have to beat it out of you?"

Amanda blinked with confusion. "I don't think I know what you're talking about."

"Rumor has it that you were sent out on assignment with Jacob on Friday night. *Late* Friday night." She waggled her eyebrows. "How'd *that* go?"

Amanda blanched. "It went...fine. Just fine. No problems."

Did the whole office know about the assignment? Would they find out what had happened between her and Jacob? After all, everyone in the office had psychic abilities to one degree or another.

She forced herself to remain calm. The compulsion to tell the truth and read the other's mind was only a manifestation of the curse. She reminded herself that abilities like that were not normal so she didn't have to worry that her secret would get out. Some empaths might be able to sense something was going on, but when wasn't there sexual tension in an office atmosphere between male and female coworkers?

"He is so delicious," Vicky said dreamily. "If Jacob Caine was lunchmeat I would eat him every single day of the week and never get sick of the taste."

Amanda twisted a nervous finger through her hair. "Lovely analogy."

"Thanks, I thought so." Vicky grinned. "You're kind of moody today, aren't you?"

Amanda laughed out loud at that. "I'm moody every day. You, of all people, should know that."

"Good point. I hope you're ready for your big party tomorrow night."

"Who's invited?"

"Just twenty or thirty of your closest friends. All really drunk and disorderly."

"So, same as usual, then." Amanda couldn't help but smile at the mental image. Damn. She would miss everybody. She could barely believe that she was finally leaving.

"Will Jacob be coming?" Vicky asked.

"Not sure."

"I hope he will."

Amanda cringed at that. She'd almost forgotten about Vicky and Jacob's date last month. The reminder of Jacob's sexual prowess did not make her feel better.

In fact, it made something akin to jealousy twist in her gut.

Why would she feel jealous of any woman that Jacob had been with before her? He was an admitted womanizer. Hot men with commitment issues usually were. It shouldn't bother her at all. Yet it did. It bothered her a *lot*.

"You should definitely try to hook up with him again," Amanda forced herself to say, and the words left a bad taste in her mouth. "You two make a cute couple."

Vicky sighed heavily.

"What?" Amanda looked up at the mournful sound.

Vicky shrugged. "I don't think that's going to happen."

"Why not?"

"You know the rumors about him being a total stud muffin? A different woman every night?"

Amanda gave her a tight smile. "Mm-hmm."

"I don't think it's true. Not completely, anyhow. I mean, I know when he first moved to town he worked his way through a lot of girls. But lately...I think he might be a little more selective. Or maybe he's just in a dating slump."

"He went out with you."

"It was only dinner. Don't tell anyone, but we didn't actually...*do* anything."

Amanda's eyes widened. "You didn't?"

Vicky set her jaw. "Not that I didn't try. I guess he just wasn't that into me."

"Wow." Amanda couldn't believe what she was hearing. She'd been sure Vicky and Jacob had slept together. And, at the time, Vicky hadn't said anything to make her think otherwise.

"It stung a bit," Vicky continued. "But I'm totally over it. I've got it bad for Patrick now."

"Our *boss*, Patrick?"

She nodded enthusiastically. "Yup."

"He's recovering from a spinal cord injury, you do realize."

"And as soon as he's mobile again I will be helping him with his rehabilitation. And by that I mean his *sexual* rehabilitation."

Amanda laughed. "I'm sure he'll be happy to hear that."

She was still thinking about what Vicky had just said. She'd believed completely that Jacob slept with any woman who even glanced in his direction. But he hadn't slept with Vicky when he'd had ample opportunity. Maybe Amanda had imagined the flush in her cheeks, the excitement from getting her hands on Jacob's irresistible, hard-muscled body.

"Speak of the devil," Vicky said.

Amanda pulled herself out of her thoughts of Jacob and his body. "What?"

"He's headed this way."

"Who?"

"Who do you think?" Vicky was looking out the door of Amanda's office. "Hey, Jacob. Looking good."

"Right back at you, Vicky," Jacob said as he stepped into Amanda's office. Then his attention was all on Amanda. "Can I speak to you in private?"

"I can take a hint," Vicky said. "I'll get back to work."

"No!" Amanda protested a little too loudly. "Please. Uh...just stay here. I have to go over my current caseload with you, anyhow. Whatever Jacob needs to say he can say now or it can wait."

"All right," Vicky replied, but she sounded uncertain.

Jacob's lips thinned. "I guess it can wait."

"Okay." Amanda forced a smile.

What is this? Jacob's thoughts were projected very clearly in her head. *Afraid to be alone with me now?*

"Yes," she said out loud, then kicked herself for her

truth-telling compulsion. Damn. Did it even work when he simply thought the question? That was so unfair.

It was like she was acknowledging her uncontrollable need to touch him. To run her hands over his beautiful body. To taste his mouth, rip open his shirt, and lick a slow line down to his...

Damn.

At the moment, she was glad that he couldn't read *her* mind.

"Please, Vicky, have a seat," she said.

Jacob groaned with obvious frustration.

Goddammit, he thought. *She's afraid to be alone with me now. How am I supposed to tell her I think I'm falling in love with her?*

Amanda's mouth went dry and her gaze shot to his. His green eyes widened. Obviously he hadn't meant her to hear that last thought.

"Amanda...I..." he began and then closed his mouth.

Vicky watched curiously. "Am I missing something here?"

"No," Amanda said quietly, looking down at her desk.

Jacob swore softly under his breath. "I'll see you around." Then he turned and left her office.

Amanda's heart thudded hard in her chest. This wasn't happening. It *wasn't.* Jacob couldn't be falling in love with her. That didn't make any sense at all. It was part of the curse. He only *thought* he was falling in love with her.

"Wow," Vicky said. "*That* was intense."

"That was nothing." Her voice was barely audible.

"Yeah, right." Vicky grinned. "Is there something between you two that I don't know about? I thought you hated the guy."

"I do." But, of course, she didn't. More lies he'd be able to see through with a well-placed question.

"Well, there is a thin line between love and hate, isn't there? All it takes is a little push to stumble over to the other side."

"It's not like that."

Vicky shrugged. "All I can say is that if I could get some guy to look at me that intensely, I'd be a happy girl."

"You're seeing things," Amanda said firmly. "Now, let's start going over my cases. Tomorrow's my last day, after all."

Vicky moved toward her and gave Amanda a big hug. "I'm going to miss you so much!"

Amanda hugged her back and felt her throat tighten. "I'll miss you, too."

"Are you absolutely sure you're not going to change your mind and stay?"

"I'm sure. Everything's in place. David will be back tomorrow before the party to help me move my stuff."

Vicky made a face. "That David. He's nice enough, I guess, but he's just so boring."

"That's your opinion. I really like him."

"*Like* him?" Vicky repeated. "I'd hope that you'd feel more than 'like' for the guy you're planning on changing your entire life for. But that's just my opinion again. All I can say is he's no Jacob Caine."

No, he wasn't.

How am I supposed to tell her I think I'm falling in love with her? Jacob's thought still echoed in her mind.

It wasn't true.

It couldn't be.

FOR THE REST of the day and night she stayed as busy as she could and found that it was possible to push thoughts of Jacob to the back of her mind. She could function.

But when she did think of him, it wasn't only about how much she was attracted to him and how he'd made her feel when they'd had sex. No, she was thinking about him beyond the physical. The fact that she liked talking to him, liked how he challenged her and made her think about things from a different point of view. She felt a strange companionship when they were alone together.

Also, this was a man who knew what it was like to be a psychic, and he didn't have a problem with it. In fact, he thought her abilities were, how did he put it? *Amazing?*

She wasn't mad at him for grilling her mother yesterday about the past. He'd made her all but admit that Amanda's father hadn't left only because he didn't want to deal with Amanda's psychic abilities.

Could it be possible? she wondered.

The thought didn't make her feel that much better about being abandoned by her dad at such a young age, but it did make her feel...*different.*

After all, his shunning of her had led to a lot of self-image issues. Maybe if she'd had two supportive parents who'd loved her unconditionally no matter how strange she was, it might have made the cruel taunts from the kids at school a little more bearable—and the nickname of Amanda the Strange wouldn't get that immediate knee-jerk reaction from her that had turned her off Jacob in the first place.

SIX YEARS at PARA. She looked around the office after she'd cleaned out her desk on Tuesday afternoon. Hard to believe so much time had passed. Everyone else had left to get ready for her party that night at O'Grady's. She felt a strange twinge in her chest then. A sense of loss. She'd miss here more than she'd realized.

You don't have to go, a little voice in her head reminded her. *You can stay here with the people who accept you exactly as you are.*

No, she'd go to the city with David. She'd make it work.

As far as she was concerned, the choice had already been made.

Besides, she hadn't even seen Jacob since he'd mentally admitted to possibly falling in love with her in her office yesterday morning. He'd kept a low profile ever since.

It was better that way. It made things a lot easier.

And this magical pull she felt toward him that had reached near-painful proportions due to his very noticeable absence would fade over time.

She sure as hell hoped it would.

So, she'd go to the party. She'd try to have a good time with her coworkers and friends. And tomorrow her new life would begin. She clutched her heavy cardboard box filled with her personal belongings against her chest and tried to ignore the lump in her throat.

"Have to say, I'm sorry to see you go," Patrick said.

Amanda jumped. She hadn't even seen him wheel up to her office doorway.

"Thanks." She smiled at him. "That means a lot."

"You're one of the best clairvoyants I've ever met, and I don't feel any shame in telling you that I'm going to have one hell of a hard time replacing you."

"I'm sure you'll find somebody."

"Maybe." He gave her a half smile. "Everybody's going to really miss you."

He was such a sweetheart. "Are you trying to make me cry?"

"Depends if you're swayed by sentimental statements or not."

"Tissues may be required."

He took a deep breath and leaned back slightly in his wheelchair. "I'm going to put this out there for you and you can do with it what you want. If you ever change your mind about this single-minded need to fit in with regular society, you're welcome to come back."

"That's not necessary," she said.

"Maybe it's not necessary, but it's still true."

"You think I'm going to get to New York, find it's too much for me, tuck my tail between my legs and run back here?"

"All I'm saying is that if you realize that there has never been anything wrong in your life to begin with, and that moving somewhere else doesn't change who you are deep down inside, then there will always be a place for you here."

The lump in her throat thickened and she had to swallow hard to get past it. She went to him, leaned over, and gave him a big hug which he returned. "I appreciate it, Patrick."

His smile widened and he shook his head. "He's right about you, you know. You are a very stubborn woman."

Her eyes widened. "Who said that?"

"Jacob."

She groaned. "Right. Well, everybody's entitled to their opinion, aren't they?"

"They are, indeed. Listen, Amanda, I wanted to tell you that I'm finished looking over the paperwork and everything's in order for the Davis house. I am authorizing the exorcism and destruction of the clock. I already told Jacob, but I thought you'd want to know."

"Oh." A chill went down her spine. She'd expected this,

of course, but it was still a bit unnerving to find out that everything was going to proceed right on schedule.

"I'll send Jacob back this week to take care of things. Maybe Vicky can go to help with the exorcism itself."

She shook her head. "I want to go."

"You? But you're through here. I'd thought you'd be happy somebody else is going to take care of it."

"I'd like to help. There's still time."

"I thought you were leaving tomorrow."

"I can delay my move for another day. David won't mind."

"He's very understanding, isn't he?" By his tone, there was no mistaking what Patrick was getting at.

Her face warmed. "I'd appreciate if you kept what you know about me and Jacob to yourself. There's no need for any gossip to get around."

"I totally agree."

"Well...good." She cleared her throat, suddenly feeling very uncomfortable. "Everything will be better once we take care of that grandfather clock."

"So you're completely convinced that the clock is the source of all evil in this situation, huh?"

"Of course I am."

"It acts as a troublesome, magical aphrodisiac and that's about it."

"Exactly." She frowned at his tone. "Why? Don't you think that, too?"

He shrugged. "I have my doubts, to tell you the truth."

"Such as?"

"Such as the fact that I found some information on Catherine Myles's aunt in some PARA historical documents. She was a witch named Rose Embry who practiced her magic out in the open over near Albany at the turn of the century and died just before the Second World War, but there was no indication of her magic ever being black or malicious in nature. I originally had the impression she sold love potions, but that wasn't exactly what it was. She specialized in spells that revealed secrets and pointed her clients to the truth in their hearts."

"The truth in their hearts? What does that mean?"

He spread his hands. "Only that Rose's wedding gift to Catherine in the form of an enchanted clock brings up a lot of unanswered questions. My guess is that she never would have wished ill on her. Perhaps she didn't approve of her marriage to an overbearing man like her niece's chosen husband, one that Catherine would have married mostly out of a need for wealth and security, but she wouldn't have helped to set in motion the events leading to her death."

"What about her servant, Nathan?" Amanda asked.

"Yes, Nathan. I must admit, I found nothing on him. But he was a man and Catherine was a woman. The clock's magic may have revealed true feelings between them that normally would have been ignored or denied due to their social differences. The aunt's truth magic just helped to peel away any reservations they might have had about engaging in a relationship, physical or otherwise."

"Is this fact or are you only speculating?" Amanda asked.

"I'm afraid I'm only speculating."

Amanda weighed what he was saying. What if the clock didn't send out a *curse* to anyone in its presence, but a *spell* to reveal hidden feelings? Like a sexy, magical truth serum making its victims admit what they really wanted and unable to fight against the desire to be together?

If that was true, then why had Catherine and Nathan been forced to haunt the house for a hundred years after their deaths, unable to be together except for an hour a day during which they couldn't even touch?

Didn't sound all that romantic to her.

"Well, after the clock is dismantled and torched it won't be an issue anymore," she said.

"So you think it'll be that easy? Burn the clock, break the spell and everyone goes back to life as usual?"

She narrowed her eyes. "What are you getting at?"

He grimaced. "Forget it. I need to keep my nose out of other people's business. It's going to get me in trouble."

"Good idea."

"However," he continued, "I think you should consider what you'll do if you still feel the same way about Jacob when there's no enchanted clock to blame your problems on."

"I thought you were going to mind your own business?"

He mock-zipped up his mouth and threw away the key. "I'm done now."

"Promise?"

"Promise. I'll see you later at O'Grady's."

She left, looking back at the office building one last time before getting in her Honda to drive home and get ready for the party.

She decided not to think about what Patrick had said, or, at least, think about it as little as possible. Life was moving forward. Time was not pausing to allow her to contemplate any other outcome. She'd go to the party, smile and have some drinks. She'd say goodbye to all of the people who turned out. Tomorrow she'd go to the Davis house and help to exorcise the ghosts—part of her job she'd done dozens of times before—and get rid of the clock once and for all.

She'd bring her own matches to start the bonfire.
And then she'd be free to start her new life.
There was no turning back now.

_11_

JACOB had considered not going to the party at all, but he'd decided to suck it up and force himself. Put on a good front. Say goodbye to Amanda all proper and politely, wish her luck with her new life, and then almost certainly get rip-roaringly drunk.

It was a plan.

He needed fresh air after being at the small pub for half an hour and emerged into the evening just as Amanda and David walked up to the entrance. He couldn't have timed it better if he'd tried.

Amanda looked incredible in a dark blue dress with a gauzy skirt that skimmed her curves and came a couple inches above her knees. She'd done her dark hair so it hung in long, soft wavy pieces, begging to be touched. Her makeup was natural, with a shiny gloss on her lips that made it difficult to look anywhere else.

He'd kissed that mouth. He knew what it tasted like. What _she_ tasted like.

His body reacted to the sight of her.

Of course, the well-dressed boyfriend next to her worked like an ice-cold shower.

David thrust out his hand. "Jacob, good to see you again."

"Yeah, you, too." He shook the man's hand. His gaze moved to Amanda.

"Thanks for coming," she said softly. "It means a lot to me."

She was going to be his undoing. He wanted to be tough, but all he really wanted to do was push David out of the way and take Amanda into his arms.

This is exactly why he'd tried to avoid falling in love with anybody for two years. There was no way he could pretend to be cool, calm and collected when he was dying inside with the need to touch her.

"My pleasure," he said. "You look beautiful tonight, Amanda."

"Thank you," she replied. She was looking directly into his eyes. Intently. Where he'd expected to see stubbornness and disinterest, he could have sworn he saw regret.

Oh, no you don't, he threw the thought at her. *You made your choice. You need to stop messing with me now.*

Her eyes turned an icy shade of blue. "I'll see you inside, David."

She brushed past them and entered the club without another word.

"Sorry," David said, a confused expression on his face. "I'm not sure what's with her tonight. She's acting very preoccupied."

Jacob pressed his lips together. "Yeah, well, I guess she has a lot on her mind right now."

"I guess she does." David got a faraway look in his eyes and then he smiled. "I think she'll love it in Manhattan. She was never meant for small-town life."

"If you say so."

"Where are you from, Jacob?"

"Seattle, originally. I moved to Mystic Ridge two years ago."

"To work for PARA?"

"That's right."

"Amanda's worked there for six years." He shook his head. "I'm amazed that after such a long time with such an unusual company she is still one of the most well-adjusted and ordinary girls I've ever known."

"Amanda's not ordinary."

David's lips quirked. "I meant it as a compliment, of course."

"Amanda is not ordinary," Jacob said again. "She's *extraordinary.*"

David frowned. "I meant no offense."

"Of course you didn't." Jacob willed himself not to get angry. He counted to ten and then twenty until the compulsion to punch David went away.

"I'm simply saying that working in a field such as paranormal investigation brings with it certain experiences that must be difficult to shake off," David continued. "Strange sights, scary situations and the like?"

"Sometimes."

"If I didn't feel that Amanda wanted a change from that life, I never would have suggested that she move to be with me."

Jacob cringed. "She's a big girl. She knows what she's doing."

"She really has no idea how wonderful she is, does she?"

"I thought you said she was ordinary."

"Ordinary isn't an insult, like I said. Amanda herself wants to be ordinary. To move away from the strange world of so-called paranormal phenomena. To be a regular, tax-paying citizen."

"I'd be willing to debate that," Jacob said.

"Would you?"

He forced a smile. "Maybe another time. But you're right. Amanda does seem to know what she wants, and she wants you, so congratulations."

"I'm a lucky man."

Yeah, you sure as hell are.

He forced any malicious thoughts away. It wasn't David's fault that Amanda was the way she was.

"I'm still not sure how she even came to work for PARA in the first place," David said.

"Could be because she's the most talented clairvoyant I've ever met," Jacob replied.

David blinked. "Clairvoyant?"

Jacob frowned at the other man's confused expression. "Yeah, clairvoyant. Medium. Able to talk to ghosts and perform exorcisms."

"She can?"

"Well, of course—" Then Jacob stopped talking. It became suddenly obvious to him that Amanda had never told David exactly what she did at PARA.

And why was that? For fear that he wouldn't approve? Of course that's what it was.

Jacob gritted his teeth. Amanda only dated so-called normal guys so she could feel normal. She'd never dated anyone at the office before, at least, that's what he'd heard. Maybe if she had, she would have realized a lot sooner that she didn't have to work so damn hard to be accepted.

David was silent for a moment, deep in thought. Jacob expected him to get angry at the news that his girlfriend was a closet ghost-whisperer.

But he didn't.

"This must be why she wants to move away and quit her

job," he said softly. "So she can leave this bizarre life behind her."

"You're very insightful." Jacob tasted the acid on his tongue.

"If she's kept this from me, it's for a very good reason. I trust her. Even though it disturbs me, I'll keep this discussion we've had between us."

"Great."

"I'm just so glad she's had friends like you to help ease her way," David said. "Quite honestly, when I saw you last night, I was a bit intimidated."

"Oh, yeah?"

David nodded. "I thought you'd become a rival for her affections. But obviously there's nothing like that between you." His previously tense face now held a smile. "If there was, you're certainly not giving me much of a fight, are you?"

If Jacob hadn't felt true emotion coming from David toward Amanda when he'd shaken his hand and gotten a mild empathic read on him, he'd probably have punched him in the nose.

"I only want what's best for her," Jacob said after a moment. "And if moving to New York and forgetting about her psychic abilities is going to make her happy, then I support her decision a hundred percent."

And it was true; despite Amanda being incredibly stubborn and frustrating, he did want her to be happy. If being "normal" was going to do that, then more power to her. Jacob would stay behind with the freaks in Mystic Ridge where he belonged.

David pulled a small blue box out of his jacket pocket and opened it up to reveal a diamond solitaire ring. "Do you think she'll like it?"

A wave of nausea swept through Jacob. It was an engagement ring. David was going to propose to Amanda.

"You're going to ask her tonight?" he asked weakly.

David nodded and put the ring back into his pocket. "I am. Even after learning she's kept secrets from me, I want us to be together."

Jacob's jaw tightened. "Well, then, if you're really the best man for her, I wish you every happiness in the world."

David shook his hand. "Thank you."

The empathic read Jacob got gave him the impression that David was filled with confidence and certainty.

Two things Jacob wasn't feeling at that moment, that was for damn sure.

SINCE Amanda had entered the pub, she'd been hugged about two dozen times. Tightly. The outpouring of emotion from her friends who'd come out tonight to say goodbye to her was enough to bring tears to her eyes.

"We're going to miss you," Lauren, a psychic who specialized in palmistry, said.

"Thanks," Amanda said, accepting yet another tight hug. "I'm going to miss you, too."

She was then shuffled off to Ben, tarot card reader extraordinaire, who actually lifted her off the ground with his bear hug and then gave her a hard kiss on her cheek.

Then somebody shoved a chocolate martini in her hand and the entire place made a collective toast in her honor.

And here she'd thought the night would be awkward. Her chest felt tight with emotion from the outpouring of best wishes for her future.

She was on her second martini when she saw Jacob and

David come into the bar. Had they been talking for that long? And about what? The thought made her nervous.

Truthfully, she'd been nervous ever since she'd gotten home that day, had a shower, and started to get ready for the night. It had taken her an eternity to pick out her outfit and accessories. Then she'd burned her finger on her curling iron. Obviously she was distracted.

When David had arrived in his Volvo to take them to the party she'd only half-heartedly kissed him. She felt horrible that the spark she'd felt between them had been all but extinguished. She wondered, frankly, if there had ever been a spark there in the first place.

Jacob sidled up next to her at the bar when her head was turned in the opposite direction. She tried to ignore his thoughts. It was easy to do at the moment. It was very noisy in the pub.

"Can I talk to you?" he asked.

She swiveled around on her stool. "Talk."

"In private."

She tensed. "Not sure that's such a good idea."

He slipped off his seat and took her hand. "Come on. I promise I won't bite." He grinned. "Not *hard,* anyhow."

She tried not to smile, but couldn't help herself. "You know Patrick has given the okay for the exorcism and destroying the clock."

"He told me."

"I'm going with you."

He raised an eyebrow. "You want to make sure there are no rocks left unturned? No clocks left unburned?"

"I didn't know you were a poet."

"You bring out my inner Shakespeare."

She felt his hand then at the small of her back. The heat

from his touch sank into her and she was very glad she was sitting down because it made her legs feel very weak and wobbly. She felt like a teenager around this guy, all awkward and vulnerable. All he had to do was touch her to make her want him. It really wasn't fair at all.

"Just five minutes of your time." He leaned closer and she felt his warm breath brush against her ear. "Before it's too late."

"Too late for what?" she replied, dismayed by how breathy her voice sounded and how good Jacob smelled.

"Amanda!" Vicky ran up to her and pulled her right off her bar stool and into a fierce hug. "You look great! I love that dress! Very New York chic, I must say."

"Thanks." She glanced at Jacob who looked unhappy that they'd been interrupted. "We'll talk later, okay?"

"Sure," he said stiffly.

Patrick moved toward her in his wheelchair and instructed the bartender to open up a case of champagne so everyone got a glass.

"To Amanda," he toasted ten minutes later. "Who knows what she wants and isn't afraid to go after it, no matter what the price."

She cringed at the knowing edge to his words as he clinked his glass against hers. "I *do* know what I want."

He raised his eyebrows. "That's exactly what I just said."

"You are a troublemaker, Patrick McKay."

He grinned. "Am I that transparent?"

"Yes, you are."

She turned to her left to see that Jacob was gone and David now stood next to her.

"Can I have your attention please?" David said, loudly enough for everyone to hear.

She was surprised. She'd expected her very normal boyfriend to keep a low profile in the middle of a crowd of psychics, even if he wasn't a true believer. She knew it made him feel uncomfortable. He'd told her as much on the drive over.

"Are you going to toast me, too?" she asked.

He smiled. "I am."

She scanned the bar to see that everyone was now paying attention to them. Even Jacob, now at the back of the crowd, looked at her. While everyone else had a smile on their face as they raised their champagne glasses, Jacob didn't look happy at all.

"From the very first moment I met Amanda," David began, "I knew that this beautiful woman was the person I wanted to spend the rest of my life with. I knew that at heart we were the same and wanted the same things— such as security and acceptance—that we had the same solid and steadfast view on the world. I was pleased when she made the decision to come work with me at my advertising company. I think she's going to fit in very well there."

He placed his glass of champagne down on the bar top and fumbled in his pocket. Amanda watched him curiously.

"She fits in very well in my life, too," he continued. "A *perfect* fit, I'd say. That's why, in front of all of her friends tonight, I'd like to ask Amanda LaGrange to marry me."

Her wide eyes moved to the diamond ring that popped up in front of her.

"David..." she began. "I...I—"

He gave her a huge grin. "You're speechless, aren't you?"

She nodded. The next moment she felt the cold metal of the ring as he slid it onto her finger.

"See? What did I tell you?" he said. "A perfect fit."

The crowd of PARA agents who'd gathered at the bar to send Amanda off on her new life cheered at their engagement.

An engagement she'd hadn't exactly agreed to yet.

She looked out at the beaming crowd to see Jacob's reaction, but he was gone. Her heart sank.

The very next moment Vicky ran up to her and gave her another hug. "Wow, I knew it was serious, but I didn't think it was this serious! That is a hell of a rock you have there. I'm so jealous!"

It was a solid five minutes of more well-wishers and hugging, but this time she was too stunned to say much. She was engaged? To David?

It was more than she'd anticipated. Moving to the city, working for him in a normal job, spending more time together—that had been one thing.

But marriage?

"I think she's going to fit in very well," David had said as part of his proposal.

She could see that life with David in his world would be the fit she'd always been searching for—the one she'd convinced herself she wanted. But now that she was trying it on for size, she found that fit more than a little bit tight and uncomfortable.

At her first opportunity, she grabbed David by his hand and pulled him out of the crowd and into a private alcove of the bar.

"Do you like your ring?" he asked.

She looked down at the two-carat engagement ring. Judging by the blue box it came in, it was from Tiffany's. "It's beautiful."

"Not as beautiful as the woman who wears it."

She closed her eyes and let out a long exhale. When she

opened her eyes, David didn't look quite as pleased by whatever expression he saw on her face.

"Is there something wrong?" he asked.

"I'm afraid there is."

"Doesn't the ring fit properly?"

"That's the problem. It fits *too* well."

He frowned. "Why would that be a problem?"

She chewed her bottom lip and tried to figure out how to properly word what she wanted to say. "It fits well on the outside, but it doesn't fit well on the inside."

"I don't understand."

Amanda felt ill. "I don't want to hurt you, David. Honestly, that's the last thing I want to do. But...but I *can't* marry you."

There. She'd said it.

His eyes widened. "What?"

She shook her head. "I care about you so much. I think you're a wonderful man, really. But I'm not in love with you."

David looked genuinely shocked. "I can't believe this."

She swallowed hard, her heart pounding a mile a minute in her chest. "I'm so sorry, David. If I'd known you were going to do this tonight I probably would have said something earlier."

"So your decision not to be with me has been a work in progress, has it?" There was an unpleasant twist now to the words.

"No. It's just...it's...it's complicated."

The corners of his mouth turned down. "Is there someone else?"

"What?" Her mouth felt dry. "Of course not."

"So this doesn't have anything to do with Jacob?"

She blanched. "He has nothing to do with this decision."

"Sure he doesn't." David's face soured. It was the first time she'd seen him look at her that way. "He told me about you, you know."

"What?"

"That you can talk to ghosts. That's why you work for PARA."

Her stomach sank. "He said that?"

"I can't believe you never told me the truth."

"I..." She swallowed. "I'm sorry. I should have."

He shook his head. "I find it all rather strange, but I would have accepted this unpleasant aspect of your life. You never even gave me the chance."

"Strange and unpleasant?"

"Of course. What else could it be?"

"And that's exactly why I never told you. Because I knew that's how you'd feel about it."

He hissed out a breath. "You're making a mistake, Amanda."

She pulled off the ring and held it out to him. "You'll find someone else. Somebody who can fit into your life perfectly and not think twice about it. Someone who's not strange or unpleasant."

His lips twisted as he accepted the ring back from her. "Is that a psychic prediction?"

She shook her head. "It's a promise. Goodbye, David."

He pocketed the ring, then with a last glare at the woman who'd turned down his offer of the perfect normal life, he left O'Grady's.

12

AMANDA TRIED HER BEST to go back to the throng of happy
people and pretend everything was okay, but it was impossible. Finding the bar increasingly stifling, she went outside
to the well-lit parking lot, sucked in great gasps of fresh air
and tried to calm down. A couple of people brushed past
her to get to their car and she forced herself to smile at them.

Then, arms crossed over her chest, she walked around
to the back of the building. She wanted to be alone for a
moment so she could collect her thoughts. An alleyway ran
behind the pub and the other downtown businesses—all
closed for the day—that it backed on to.

Other than the slight throb of music she could hear
coming from inside the pub, the alley was silent. She felt
a warm breeze move over her bare legs.

What had she just done? A part of her was mightily pissed
that she'd turned down David's proposal. Being married to
a man like him would give her a solid, secure foundation for
the rest of her life. It sounded good enough in theory.

But it wasn't. She didn't love David. If there was one
thing she believed, no matter what, it was that love and
marriage went together. Despite what had happened with
her mother and father, she held on to that particular fairy
tale with a very firm grip.

"Congratulations on your engagement," a voice pierced through her thoughts.

Her eyes widened and she looked up to see it was Jacob, who stood a dozen feet away from her in the otherwise empty back alley—just far enough to be out of reach of her mind-reading ability. She hadn't realized he was there until he spoke.

The moon was full that night and it shone down on them with a silver light. The area was empty except for the two of them. She noticed his black Mustang was parked to the right in a small, vacant employee parking area belonging to the local bookshop.

He took a few steps closer to her.

Be a man. His self-directed thoughts were now very hard to ignore. *Pretend it doesn't make a difference to you either way.*

It was best that Jacob continued to think she was engaged. It would make everything much easier.

"Thank you," she finally replied.

His brow lowered. "You're not inside with your husband-to-be, toasting your wonderfully average futures."

She looked at him sharply. "Are you making fun of me?"

He paced back and forth in front of her. "Everybody pulls out all the stops to have a regular, normal life. Sounds like the perfect 1950s sitcom to me. Very exciting stuff."

"You're upset."

He stopped moving, then laughed at that and it sounded hollow. "Strangest damn thing, but I'll admit it. I am upset."

"Any specific reason, or just upset in general?"

"Purely selfish reasons and nothing I'm particularly proud of."

She looked over at the black car parked in the shadows

and saw that the driver's side door was open. She'd be willing to bet that he'd been about to leave when she had inadvertently interrupted him in her quest for fresh air.

She chewed her bottom lip. "I really should get back—"

He closed the remaining space between them and shut off any further words with a kiss that she didn't even attempt to resist. His tongue swept into her mouth as the kiss deepened and became more passionate. Her hands were in his hair, on the sides of his face, moving down to his chest, where she finally managed to force him back a bit.

"Whoa," she said breathlessly.

He had the audacity to look proud of himself. "You taste so good."

"I need to get back to the party. They're going to wonder where I went."

"I've been thinking, Amanda, about everything that's happened between us."

She blinked. "And what have you been thinking?"

"That I'm glad it happened. I'm glad we've had the chance to get to know each other better."

"Is that so?"

He nodded, his dark, sexy gaze never leaving hers. It made things low in her belly ache with need.

"I tried to resist," he said. "I gave you some time alone to figure things out. But I know that it's not going to work. And I frankly don't give a good God damn if you're engaged to some other guy, I can't get you out of my head. If that makes me a selfish bastard, then so be it."

"But, the curse—"

His jaw set. "Right, the curse."

"Did Patrick tell you his hypothesis of what the curse actually is?"

"No." His expression held guarded curiosity. "What did he say?"

She nervously looked around, expecting to be interrupted by someone from her party at any moment, but there was no one but the two of them. "He said he thought it might be a spell to reveal true feelings. Catherine's aunt was a witch who apparently was a bit of a matchmaker."

"Interesting." He was quiet for a moment. "So when two people meant to be together get in the path of this clock, they can't ignore how they really feel any longer?"

She shifted her feet. "He was speculating only."

"You think?"

"Patrick is great and smart, and I know he cares about what happens to us, but that doesn't mean he's necessarily right about this."

"So you still don't think this could be real, what we have between us?"

She raised her eyebrows. "This insanity that makes us act like sex addicts?"

"Yeah," he grinned. *"That."*

"No, I don't think it's real." She made a move to walk away from him. She'd wanted privacy so she could clear her head. Well, her head was clear and now she wanted to go back to the buzz and activity—and, well, *safety*—of the party she could hear muffled through the thick brick back wall of the pub. She couldn't deal with this. It was too much and the confusing emotions were beginning to choke her.

"If you're worried I'm going to say something to David about us, you don't have to be."

Her mouth was dry. "You mean like how you told him I'm clairvoyant?"

He sighed. "I was just attempting small talk with your

perfect fiancé. How was I supposed to know you'd never shared that particular detail of your life with him?"

"You weren't." She couldn't very well blame Jacob for that. It had been her own mistake that finally came back to bite her in the end.

She turned away from him.

"Amanda—" Jacob captured her hands in his before she could get far and brought them to his lips. "Maybe this *is* only magic. Hell, it would make more sense then. I've never felt anything so strong, so hard to resist, in my entire life. Try to tell me you don't feel the same way."

She bit her lip instead of answering.

He studied her for a moment, and then looked down at her hands. Most specifically her left hand, and he rubbed his thumb over her ring finger. "Where's the bling?"

"The what?"

"The bling. The engagement ring. Why aren't you wearing it?"

She felt the compulsion to tell the truth well up inside of her. "Because I said no to him." She grimaced. "Shit."

His eyes widened. "You said *no?*"

She couldn't help but nod her head. Damn that need to tell the truth! As long as Jacob phrased something in the form of a question, she had to be completely honest with him. It was like a whacked episode of *Jeopardy.*

She was definitely doomed.

JACOB honestly couldn't believe it. He'd been certain, absolutely no-doubt-about-it certain, that Amanda and David were engaged. As soon as David pulled out the ring in the bar, he'd left. He hadn't waited around to hear the verdict, since he was sure it would be a yes.

The fact that it wasn't completely stunned him.

He knew that she wouldn't have told him the truth if he'd given her any other choice. Why was that? If she'd turned David down, the man who represented everything to her that Jacob himself wasn't—i.e., a normal guy who didn't give her any trouble—then what did that mean? Was she admitting that it wasn't what she wanted anymore?

There was only one way to find out.

He pressed up against her and felt her tense, but she didn't try to pull away from him. "I have a couple more questions for you, Amanda."

A sliver of dread moved through her gaze. "Please, Jacob, don't make me say anything."

"Anything you might regret?"

She nodded.

He flinched. He didn't want to force her to do anything. The thought was painful to him. "Why would you regret the truth? That's what I'm getting at here. All I want is the truth."

"The truth when I'm feeling all vulnerable doesn't mean it's the real truth."

"What are you, a lawyer?" She was so logical about everything he had to grin. That only succeeded in making her angry.

"No, not a lawyer," she answered truthfully. "Let go of me."

He did immediately and she let out a sigh of relief.

However, he wasn't finished yet.

"Do you want me?" he asked, bracing himself for her reply.

"Yes." She cringed and glared at him. "Please stop that."

A swell of dark pleasure moved through him at the answer. He studied her for a long moment. His gaze flitted from her beautiful but strained face down her luscious body, her long bare legs, then back up again.

He struggled to breathe as he willed himself to ask the question he desperately needed the answer to. "Are you in love with me?"

"Yes." Immediately, her eyes bugged with shock at her reply.

Yes? She'd said yes?

He was so stunned by the answer that he couldn't speak for a moment.

Amanda was in love with him. She'd answered truthfully—she had to. He wasn't sure what answer he'd expected, but he hadn't expected one so certain and decisive.

She looked distraught. "*Dammit,* Jacob. Why are you doing this?"

"Do you hate me for making you answer that question?" he managed.

"No," she replied, averting her gaze.

Amanda tried to keep her emotions in check. To have everything she was feeling out on the table must have made her feel incredibly exposed.

"I'm sorry," he said. "I shouldn't be doing this. It's not really very fair, is it?"

"No, it's not." She swallowed and her eyes locked with his.

"Do you want to go back to the party right now?"

She shook her head. "Not yet."

That truthful answer was a surprise. Even more of a surprise when she placed her hands flat against his chest. Her full, red lips were slightly parted and there was no mistaking the expression of desire on her face.

He ran his hands down the sides of her waist and hips before he raised his gaze to hers again.

"Do you want me to make love to you right now? Right here?"

"Yes."

"We're alone right now, but anyone could walk back here at any moment."

"I don't care." She touched his face, his cheekbones, forehead, jawline, his lips. The heat from her fingers seared into him.

"Say it out loud," he breathed. "Just so we don't have any misunderstandings."

"Make love to me, Jacob. Right here. Right now."

His mouth met hers again and he kissed her long and slow and it grew deeper and harder. His hard cock strained painfully against the front of his jeans.

This wasn't normal, this way he burned for her. It wasn't average, the way his body ached for her. It was magical. He wanted her more than any other woman he'd ever known before and the thought actually scared him with its intensity.

She could hear the truth of his thoughts, he saw it in her eyes.

"I want you," she managed. "So much."

She made a small sound of protest when he pulled away from her touch.

"What's wrong?" she asked breathlessly.

"Nothing," he said. "Everything. Damn, I don't know anymore. I don't know what's right, what's wrong. What's real and what's not. And I don't really care."

He took her hand and led her over to his car, kissing her deeply as his hands moved up her warm silky thighs under her dress. She gasped against his lips as he brushed his fingers against her panties. He couldn't help but grin.

"You're already wet for me," he observed.

She just nodded.

He glanced around to ensure they were still alone, then made short work of the panties, pulling the lacy bit of fabric down her long, lean legs. She pressed up against the hood of his car. He didn't normally like it when anybody touched the machine, let alone sat on it, but he was willing to make a very big exception for Amanda.

He pushed up the gauzy material of her dress to bare her smooth legs. She didn't protest at all as his hands moved up her thighs, followed by his mouth as he left a trail of kisses on her creamy flesh. He pushed the dress up high enough to expose her glistening sex to the night air and silver moonlight.

"Damn," he said, overwhelmed by the feel of her, the scent of her, and when he swept his tongue over her hot sweet core and she bucked against him, the desire only grew. She was soft and wet and tasted like dark honey. He moved his tongue over her again, feeling her hands clutching at his shoulders and upper back.

She began making a low keening sound deep in her throat that only served to make him go slower, tasting her deeply, before sliding his tongue along her inner lips and circling her clit. His hands kneaded her thighs, pressing them wider apart, before he moved his right hand to her wet cleft, slowly sliding two fingers inside her while he continued to stroke his tongue over that delicious pink bud.

"Jacob!" she gasped, and then let out a harsh cry as he felt a shudder ripple through her entire body.

He wanted more. He couldn't stop. He couldn't get enough. But she pulled his face up to hers and kissed him, openmouthed, wet and deep.

"I guess I can't pretend that I don't want you anymore," she whispered. "The proof is in the mind-shattering orgasm."

"You can pretend," he replied hoarsely. "But I might not believe you."

She kissed his mouth and chin and down his throat, working her hands up under his shirt. He was so hard it was painful, and when she unzipped his pants and pulled him free, he nearly came as she slid her tongue over the head of his shaft.

He swore loudly and he saw her smile at that.

"Not just dreaming now, are we?" she asked.

He shook his head, feeling the sweat breaking out on his forehead. He tried to control himself as she took him in her mouth, sucking and licking him in slow, even strokes from the base to tip. She held him firmly in one hand while the other caressed his balls. When she ran her tongue over them each in turn he almost exploded.

"You're killing me," he groaned.

"Are you saying that you like this?" She grinned and looked up at him.

She was killing him, and she was finding it funny. That sounded like Amanda. He squeezed his eyes shut tightly and let the pleasure she was giving him wash over him. He'd had no idea how talented that little mouth of hers was. He'd had a brief preview in their shared dream, but that hadn't come close to preparing him for the real thing.

Since he didn't want to finish this way, although it was definitely a great way to begin, he leaned over and coaxed her up to her feet.

"Problem?" she asked. Her face was flushed but her eyes sparkled with life. She knew what she did to him. Obviously the ability to read his mind while she had him in her mouth was a definite advantage for her.

"No problem," he breathed, and kissed her again. He'd never been so hard in his life.

He moved her so that she was facing away from him and toward the trunk of his car, and then pressed a hand against her back. She leaned forward without protest. He pulled her skirt up over her hips.

"Jacob—" She looked over her shoulder at him. Her voice was breathy with need. "Please. I need you inside of me."

He was all thumbs as he fumbled for a small foil packet from his wallet, ripped it open and rolled the condom on. Then he positioned himself against her and heard her moan in pleasure as he slowly sheathed himself inside her.

He was sure she wouldn't be getting a very good reading on his thoughts at the moment because he currently was incapable of any coherent thought. She felt better than anything. *Anyone.* He honestly didn't think that he could ever grow weary of how she made him feel.

He brought her up so that her back pressed against his chest, and he slid his hands down the front of her dress, pleased that she was braless so he could take her full breasts in his hands as he thrust into her heat, in and out, in and out.

He swore again, trying to hold back his climax for as long as he could. "Amanda," he groaned. "You feel so good, I can't take it."

"Yes," she gasped in reply. "Don't stop. Please don't stop."

But he couldn't hold back for much longer. After only a couple of more ecstasy-streaked minutes he reached the end of his restraint and felt the dark waves of pleasure roll through him like a runaway train. He let out a hoarse cry as he came and collapsed against her, still touching her, still needing to be close to her.

Her mouth found his and she kissed him for a full minute before pulling away a little. She nibbled at her bottom lip and actually managed to look bashful.

"What's with the innocent act?" he asked, with a weary smile.

She shook her head and kissed him again. "I...I never would have done anything like that right here, right next to O'Grady's...but, I couldn't stop myself. It's always so intense with you."

"I'll take that as a compliment."

She smiled a little. "Especially when I give in to it instead of trying to resist the magic." She touched his face, and slid her thumb over his bottom lip. Her gaze was soft. "I think I'm definitely going to miss that."

Her lips brushed against his again and he already felt the stirrings of another erection, but he pushed those sensations away for the moment. "What do you mean you're going to miss that?"

She smiled and moved her hand down to take his semi-erect cock in her hand and stroked it slowly. "I'm going to miss the way you make me feel. How you feel inside of me." Another kiss. "I want you again. Right now."

He straightened up and stepped away from her, then tucked himself back into his pants and buttoned his shirt.

Her smile faltered and she pushed her dress back in place so it fell to just above her knees. "What's wrong?"

"You still don't think this is real?"

"No." The truth left her full lips and his heart sank.

"I see."

She frowned at him. "You *know* this is a spell."

"Right." He blinked hard and tried to ignore the rising frustration in his chest. "So you broke up with your boyfriend, refused his proposal, all because of a magic spell that makes you horny for my body."

Her cheeks flushed. "You think I broke up with him because of you?"

He scowled at her. He didn't have to reply. She easily read everything that currently rushed through his mind.

She clenched her teeth. "For your information, it had very little to do with you, Jacob. I broke up with him because I realized that I wasn't in love with him. I can't marry somebody I'm not in love with."

"You said you were in love with me," he said. "Would you marry me?"

"Yes," she replied, then swore under her breath. "Why do you do that?"

"Just trying to figure out the truth."

"Okay, Jacob, yes. *Yes.* I am in love with you. I want you so much I can barely function." Her voice broke a little. "And at this very moment I would agree to spend the rest of my life with you."

He studied her fixedly. "But?"

"But the only reason we feel like this is because of a spell."

"So it's not real?"

"That's what I've been trying to say." She inhaled deeply and then let out a long, shuddery breath. "And when we go to the house tomorrow and fix things, there is a very high likelihood that all of this will go away."

"And then what happens?" he pressed. "We're just supposed to ignore each other and pretend nothing ever happened between us?"

"It'll be easy since I'll be in New York."

He took a step back. "I thought you broke up with David."

"I did." She licked her lips in an obviously nervous gesture. "But I'm still moving there. It doesn't change anything. Besides, I wasn't going there just to be with David, I was going there to start a new life. As soon as we take care of the ghosts and the clock, I'll be leaving."

Why this took him by surprise, he wasn't exactly sure. He supposed that finding out that she and David were no longer together had led him to assume that she would be staying in Mystic Ridge and keeping her job. But nothing had changed. Nothing at all.

"Why wait until tomorrow?" he asked. "Let's go tonight and get it over with."

She was silent for a moment. "Tonight?"

He nodded. "It's only nine-thirty. We get in my car and drive to the Davis house. In five hours we'll be back and it'll all be over. You'll be free, and I promise not to bother you ever again."

Her expression twisted for a moment, and he could have sworn he saw tears brimming in her perfectly madeup eyes, but then she managed to compose herself. "I think that's a very good idea. But, I need candles and salt for the exorcism. And we can't forget the cleansing oil for the clock."

"All of that's already in my trunk," he said. "Ready for tomorrow."

"Matches?"

"I have a lighter."

She blinked slowly. "But, if you've been drinking at the party you shouldn't be driving anywhere."

"Haven't even had a beer yet. I was saving it up. Thought I'd get blitzed later and walk home. Hell, I still might." In fact, he was a little sorry he was so acutely sober at the moment.

She was obviously out of excuses. "Okay, then let's go."

Amanda's gaze moved around the general area, seemingly searching for something.

"If you're looking for your panties—" Jacob suppressed an evil grin "—I'm afraid that'll be two pair I'll need to write you an IOU for now. Whoops."

She glared at him, but didn't reply to that. Instead, she got in the passenger side and arranged her skirt around her knees. "It's probably a good idea if you try to keep your thoughts to yourself on the way up. It's a long drive, after all."

Yeah, like that was going to happen. She didn't want anything to do with him? She thought this was all one big *bibbidi-bobbidi-boo?* She would get to listen to every damn thing that went through his mind about her. And he might just throw in some of his personal fantasies involving handcuffs and whipped cream just to mix it up a bit.

13

"THAT'S RIGHT," JACOB said into his cell phone as they sped along the highway. "I'll text you when we're done. Don't worry. We'll be fine."

He'd placed a call to let Patrick know what they were planning on doing. Amanda felt bad about abandoning her going-away party, but it was too late to turn back now so she could suck down a couple of more martinis and finish hugging everyone in a three-mile radius.

No, she'd definitely had enough one-on-one physical contact for the night. She crossed her legs and tried to forget about the fact that she was presently not wearing any underwear.

This trip could have waited until tomorrow. It probably *should* have waited until tomorrow.

She glanced at Jacob as he listened to whatever Patrick was telling him. He didn't look at her, in fact, he hadn't looked directly at her in the hour since she'd gotten in the car.

He was pissed off. She honestly couldn't say that she blamed him.

She tried desperately not to pay attention to Jacob's thoughts. Even though he tried to mask his true feelings with a montage of flashy, sexy images, she could see through to the raw emotion underneath.

But seriously, how had he expected this to play out? That they'd end up together? That an enchanted clock had pointed both of them in the direction of true love?

He was a relative newbie, but she'd been in the paranormal investigation business long enough to know the difference between reality and *magic-enhanced* reality. There were many different enchanted and cursed objects she'd uncovered over the years, and many spells of varying strengths had swept over her. They'd all faded sooner or later.

Anything that felt as strong as what she felt for Jacob at the moment had to be fake.

Sure, they'd known each other for two years, but they hadn't spent very much time in each other's company. After that first meeting—

She recalled their gazes locking from across the floor. It had been at O'Grady's as well, hadn't it? She'd felt that sudden, irresistible, sexual attraction to him—what some people might call love at first sight. That hadn't been real either because as soon as they'd spoken to each other it had faded.

No, *faded* wasn't the right word. It had been pushed out of the way by the wrong thing said at the wrong time. She'd convinced herself that she strongly disliked him, even *hated* him, based on that first meeting.

She flicked another glance at his profile as he kept his attention on the road ahead of them. She'd definitely been aware of him in the office for two years. *Painfully* aware. The man was attractive and undeniably sexy, after all. She wasn't blind.

But they'd been forced to work one-on-one for the first time on Friday night. That was only—she counted in her head—four nights ago.

It was as if a decade had gone by since then. She felt as if she knew Jacob better than anyone she'd ever known before in her life. Sure, it was mostly to do with her being able to wade through his thoughts, but it was more than that. There was a connection between them that went way beyond the physical.

Although the physical was pretty nice, too.

It was all just part of the spell.

What if it isn't? a little annoying voice poked at her. *What if this is real?*

"Thinking about me?" he asked, his voice breaking the silence in the car.

"Yes," she replied immediately and then pressed her lips together. Reading minds was handy, but compelling someone to tell the truth was embarrassing.

His attention left the road for a split second as he glanced at her. "Patrick thinks we're being rash."

"He said that?"

He nodded.

"Does he want us to come back?"

"No, but he warned us to be careful."

She crossed her arms. "The ghosts won't be a problem. I actually think they'll welcome the opportunity to leave their misery behind."

"How exactly do you exorcise them?"

"Don't you know these things already?"

"If I did, I wouldn't be asking you." He flicked her a glance. "I've never been sent out on any exorcisms before. Since I'm an empath, ghost-busting isn't exactly my specialty. Is it anything like in *The Exorcist?*"

She couldn't help but laugh. "No. That's demonic possession. Ghosts are a bit different."

"How?"

"Their ties to this world are less strong, so it takes less effort to remove them. Actually, every clairvoyant I know has a different method. Some stick to the books, but I've found that lighting three candles, surrounding the candles with a small circle of salt—well, that will draw the ghost to me. I have an incantation I've memorized—a Latin one. It cleanses the house and makes it completely inhabitable to the ghosts."

"What happens to the ghost then?"

This was all common knowledge to her. "Most of the time it gives them the push they need to go on to the after-life, kind of like scraping a splattered bug off your wind-shield. But if they're very resistant to leaving, then an exorcism will decimate the spirit completely."

"Decimate?"

"Yeah, obliterate. Make it as if it never existed."

"Sounds harsh."

She shrugged. "If the spirits are evil they can be dan-gerous. It's the best way."

"But Catherine and Nathan aren't evil."

"No, they aren't. But bottom line, PARA is a business. We work for our clients. If we didn't do what they wanted, within limits, then we wouldn't be able to stay in business very long, would we?"

"*We?*" he repeated. "Remember, you quit. You're basi-cally a freelancer now."

"Right." She'd forgotten about that for a moment.

"What'll you do in New York?" he asked. "I assume you're not going to take the job at David's ad agency anymore, are you?"

She shook her head. "I can do something else. I have

some money saved up, a nest egg to last me long enough to figure things out."

"Very smart."

"My mother raised me to be practical."

"*Practical* is definitely a word I'd use to describe you, Amanda. And your mother, too, for that matter."

She cringed at the subtle insult, but then thought about it for a moment. "I know you probably think she's a horrible person, keeping the truth about my father from me for all of those years, but she's only been trying to protect me. She's not a bad mother."

He was silent for a moment. "You know her better than I do."

"I'm not saying that it makes what she did right."

"No, it doesn't." The angry twist of his lips slowly changed to curl up with borderline amusement. "She really couldn't stand me."

"Of course not. You're one of the psychic freaks who have corrupted her daughter all of these years."

He raised an eyebrow. "*Card-carrying* psychic freak, and proud of it."

She smiled at that. "You really don't look like a freak."

"I appreciate that." He glanced at her out of the corner of his eye. "And just for the record, neither do you."

She reached out to touch him, she couldn't help herself. She slid her fingers through his dark hair. "I really think you mean that."

He captured her hand with his and brushed his lips against it. Then he blinked and looked at the road again. "Another hour and we'll be there. I'm making good time."

"I feel like I've been apologizing all night long, but I want you to know how sorry I am, Jacob."

"Sorry? For what?"

She swallowed past the lump in her throat. "That this couldn't be real."

The softness that had grown in his gaze hardened and his jaw tightened. "Right. Can't forget that for a second, can we?"

She frowned. "I don't want to fight with you."

"Me neither. So maybe it would be better if we just don't say anything else for the rest of the ride."

She licked her dry lips. "Fine with me."

She'd already called the owner of the haunted house, Sheila Davis, to let her know that they'd be performing the cleansing ritual as requested. Ms. Davis had been curt and unfriendly, but she did seem pleased that everything was going according to plan and ahead of schedule.

"The sooner I can sell this house, the better," she'd told Amanda before ending the call.

The cold way she looked at such a beautiful, historic property made Amanda flinch a little. Ms. Davis was going to take every penny she'd get from it and spend it on that shiny new condo in Chicago rather than attempting to live there, or even refurbish the place to give it the respect it deserved.

She supposed she couldn't fault the woman that much. It sounded a lot like what she was doing herself.

But moving to New York would grant her everything she'd ever wanted. She'd settle in before too long, find a great apartment, meet new friends, get a new job—and eventually start dating.

But she couldn't even think about something like that right now.

Finally, after what felt like an eternity—although Jacob

had turned on the radio and blasted some loud music which helped distract her a little bit—they pulled up in front of the Davis house.

"So what's the game plan?" Jacob asked without enthusiasm.

"We go in, I give Catherine and Nathan one more chance to leave of their own free will, explaining to them what will happen if they refuse. If they give us a hard time, I will exorcise them."

"Will it take long?"

"A couple of minutes. I just have to light the candles, spread the salt and read the incantation. Easy."

"Can I read it if necessary?"

She shook her head. "It has to be somebody like me. Otherwise it would take a really long time and more accessories would be required—like crucifixes and holy water—"

"So you're a real, honest to goodness, ghostbuster."

She shrugged. "It's rare, I guess, to be able to do what I do."

"Which is what makes you so special."

She turned to look at him, but he'd already averted his gaze to open up the driver's-side door.

"So you do your ghostbusting," he continued, "and then we'll tear that clock apart. Hell, who knows? We might make it back to O'Grady's for last call."

"You never know."

He pushed open the door and got out. "Come on, LaGrange. Let's not wait another minute. Let's get it done, get out and then we'll both be free to go our separate ways."

He seemed to call her by her last name when he was either amused with her or annoyed. She didn't have a hard time figuring out which he was at the moment.

A glance at her bangle-style watch told her it was a few minutes after eleven o'clock. Perfect timing, actually. Since the ghosts were free to roam the house between eleven and twelve, there would be no need to exert herself in summoning them.

No, I've exerted quite enough energy tonight, she thought, pushing away the immediate blast of desire at the memory of what had happened between her and Jacob outside the bar. She'd really been far gone to have sex with him somewhere anybody could have walked by and seen them in flagrante delicto.

She chewed her bottom lip. Why did that sound so exciting to her?

"You coming?" Jacob called to her.

Considering she didn't even accept Amanda's strange abilities, her mother definitely would never approve of somebody like Jacob. Even if she and Jacob were a regular couple, her mother would hate him. He was way too opinionated and too unpredictable.

She got out of the car and Jacob handed her a duffel bag with the candles and salt inside. He used the key provided by Ms. Davis to open the front door, and flicked on a light in the hallway.

"Déjà vu," Jacob said, glancing around at the familiar surroundings.

"Hard to believe it was only four days ago we were here last."

"A lot has happened."

"To say the least."

His lips curled into a wry smile. "Don't worry. It's almost over."

Before she could say anything in reply to that—

although she had no idea what—he said, "I'm going to find the bathroom. I didn't drink any booze at O'Grady's, but I did knock back about three sodas."

"Too much information. Go."

He grinned and took off down the hall.

Amanda tried to compose herself, put everything out of her mind except the task at hand. She spent a minute or two moving through the hall and admiring the crown molding, the original flooring, the hand-stitched area rugs. The history of the place oozed out of every crevice and she could picture Catherine living here when she was alive, throwing dinner parties and entertaining her wealthy husband's friends and business associates.

She felt the sadness there, too, of a woman who was in an unhappy marriage and more than likely trapped financially. Women a hundred years ago rarely walked out on their husbands simply because of a loveless relationship.

Women were much more practical back then. In a way she admired their fortitude. In another way, she saw the despair of not having many other choices.

Except, perhaps, having a passionate affair with a handsome servant.

"Hello again."

Amanda jumped and turned around slowly to see that Catherine stood behind her. The spirit glowed in the otherwise dark room with an inner light. At first glance she looked alive, unless you looked closely to see she was slightly transparent.

"Hello," Amanda replied.

"You've returned?"

Amanda nodded. "We have."

"We? Is your handsome gentleman with you again?"

"He is. And where is yours?"

"I don't know where Nathan is right now." Catherine suddenly became wary. "Why is it that you've returned here?"

"A couple of reasons."

"The last I saw of you, you were in the room upstairs with the clock as it struck midnight."

"You remember correctly."

"Did anything...happen? Between you and your gentleman?"

"You could say that."

"You felt an overwhelming passion for him?"

"In a manner of speaking." Amanda swallowed hard. Discussing her sex life with a dead woman wasn't exactly how she'd expected to spend this evening.

Catherine frowned. "I have seen others in the presence of the clock at the midnight hour, but very few have succumbed to its magic. I wonder why that is?"

This grabbed Amanda's attention immediately. "There were others?"

"Yes. Only one other couple that I can remember were swept away by the enchantment. Others simply left and were not moved in the slightest. At those times I believed that it no longer worked, that my aunt's spell had worn off. But you and your gentleman—"

"It hasn't worn off yet," Amanda finished. "That's one of the reasons we're back. We need to destroy the clock to break the spell."

Conflicting emotions washed over Catherine's face. "I wonder if that will free me from my deep and unnatural need for Nathan."

"So you really, truly don't believe you're in love with him," Amanda said.

"I am a practical woman," Catherine said. "I married not for love, but for a solid place in society. Obviously, emotion plays little part in how I lived my life. What I felt...what I *feel*...for Nathan goes beyond any fantasy I ever had about what love is. How could that possibly be real?"

Amanda's chest tightened. Was she looking in a mirror? This woman sounded exactly like her—denying the possibility that what she felt deep in her heart was the real thing. Instead of making her feel a true kinship with Catherine, it only served to make her angry. She could tell the other night when Catherine and Nathan looked at each other that what they felt was real. Catherine's insistence that it wasn't was more than a little annoying.

Nathan believed it was love, but Catherine refused to accept it as anything but the result of a magic spell.

Interesting.

"Is there another reason that you're here again?" Catherine asked. "Other than the destruction of my aunt's clock?"

Amanda nodded slowly. "The new owner of the house is concerned about your continued presence here. She is uncomfortable owning a haunted house."

"Unpleasant shrewish woman?" Catherine asked. "Red hair? Changed the linens in the upstairs bedrooms?"

"That's the one."

"You can let her know that we will strive to make our existence here as quiet as possible."

"You gave her a firm push out of the house a couple of times. Kind of freaked her out."

Catherine gave her a genuine smile that showed off her beauty. "Perhaps."

Amanda wasn't smiling. "I'm afraid that keeping a low

profile isn't an option. And since your curse traps you here, you can't leave of your own free will." She swallowed. "I'm going to have to exorcise you."

She wondered if she'd have to explain what that meant to Catherine, but the ghost's eyes widened with obvious knowledge and she began to shake her head.

"No," Catherine said in a choked voice. "Please. You can't."

"I have no choice."

"I know what will happen. We'll be gone. We won't be able to be together." She let out a shaky gasp. "I can't be away from him. It's bad enough that I can't touch him, but I can't lose him completely!"

Before Amanda was able to say anything else, Catherine came at her quickly and pushed her—the anger and panic she felt at the threat of being exorcised enough to give her physical and tangible strength. Amanda fell over on her ankle and hit her head on the carved-wood armrest of the antique sofa, which knocked her out cold.

However, instead of the blackness of unconsciousness, she saw something else entirely.

14

AMANDA was upstairs in the bedroom where she and Jacob had found the clock. It was different this time. Catherine was also in the room. But instead of being mostly transparent, the girl was solid. And she looked upset.

Who was the woman with her? Darker blond hair than Catherine's, older, but still beautiful. There was wisdom in her eyes.

It was her aunt, Amanda suddenly knew without any doubt. Rose Embry. The witch.

Was she dreaming this?

"Catherine—" Concern twisted in Rose's voice. "You don't have to marry him if you don't want to."

"I do, and I'm going to," Catherine replied.

"You've been crying."

She shook her head. "Tears of happiness."

"Excuse me," Amanda ventured, but the next moment Catherine walked right through her as if she wasn't even there.

She was having a vision. It was the most vivid one she'd experienced yet.

Rose's expression was filled with understanding. "I feel your pain, Catherine."

"I love you, Aunt, but this isn't any of your business. My

parents are thrilled, everyone's here and they're ready for the ceremony to begin. I can't very well turn back now."

"Do you love him?" Rose asked tightly. "This man you're committing the rest of your life to?"

Catherine sighed. "I know what this is all about. It's about Edmund, isn't it?"

Rose cringed. "Why would you say that?"

"Because you were lucky enough to experience a true and everlasting love with Edmund you can't imagine anyone marrying for more practical reasons than that. Well, I know that you loved Edmund, but it doesn't make any difference."

Amanda could see pain enter Rose's expression.

"I loved him and I lost him. The short time we had together was the most wonderful of my life. He was my soul mate."

Catherine's lips thinned. "I'm surprised you don't try conjuring his spirit up in that silly crystal ball of yours."

"He has moved beyond this realm or believe me I would do anything for the chance to see him again." Rose breathed out shakily. "What about Nathan?"

Catherine froze. "What about him?"

"Don't play coy with me, Niece. I've seen the way you look at him and how he looks at you. You're in love with him."

"With a *butler?*" Catherine repeated, incredulously. "That's impossible."

"Why? Because he doesn't fit the mold of what you consider a proper husband? Because he doesn't have the mountain of money your fiancé has? He is a man, a very handsome man, and when he looks at you I can see the rest of the world disappears for him."

"I will admit that he is very attractive, but there is nothing else there."

"Are you having an affair with him?"

Catherine gasped. "Of course not."

"Will you in the future?"

Catherine didn't speak for a very long time. "This conversation is extremely inappropriate on my wedding day, Aunt."

"You're right. But there seems to be no one else who will discuss such matters with you, Catherine. Nathan attends to you, he hangs on your every word. It is clear to me that his feelings for you run much deeper than those of an employee to the future wife of his employer."

"I shall not discuss this any further."

At that moment, Nathan walked past the room and glanced in. His blue eyes widened as he saw Catherine in her ivory-colored, beaded wedding gown.

His head lowered. "I apologize. I didn't mean to stare."

Rose's lips curled as she noticed the immediate flush come to her niece's face from the attention of the tall, attractive young man.

"Please, Nathan," Rose said. "Come in here for a moment. I need your opinion on something."

"Aunt," Catherine snarled under her breath. "Please don't."

But Nathan obeyed the order and entered the room to stand at the doorway with his hands clasped behind the waistcoat of his butler's uniform.

"Doesn't my niece look lovely today?" Rose asked.

With a tortured expression, Nathan raised his gaze to sweep slowly and appreciatively over Catherine's body. Their eyes met and locked and there was no mistaking the longing there for both of them.

And suddenly it was as if Amanda could read Rose's thoughts and sense all of her emotions. Catherine's aunt was certain these two were soul mates. It wasn't a guess, it wasn't wishful thinking, it was the truth.

Curious people willing to pay her fee would come to her and she would help lead them toward their soul mates, if they were lucky enough to have one in the world. She couldn't do all the work. The subjects themselves had to come halfway, but a little push helped move them in the right direction.

Which was how she'd decided on the perfect wedding gift. She glanced over at it in the corner of the room. A beautiful ebony grandfather clock.

Only it wasn't any normal clock.

The last thing Rose planned to do was to try to stop the wedding. She knew it would happen. But it didn't change anything.

And perhaps the clock would appear completely benign when in the presence of Bernard and his lovely young wife. It would keep time and chime at the hour. But it would be waiting patiently for the right opportunity to work its special magic.

If Nathan and Catherine truly were soul mates, a very subtle spell would waft over them at the stroke of midnight. A spell that would make them see that their love, while hidden, could not be ignored.

Rose felt certain it would work.

The magic brought with it some risk, but she was certain that Catherine and Nathan, once given the opportunity to be together body and soul, would embrace it completely.

If they didn't...there *might* be a few complications.

The spell hinged on their mutual acceptance of what they felt for each other, but if they didn't accept it...well...

Quite honestly, Rose didn't know what the consequences might be.

But she did hope for the best.

15

THE LAST THING Jacob expected to see when he emerged from the bathroom was a ghost, considering the fact that he couldn't see ghosts, and never had before in his life.

"You're here to exorcise us, aren't you?" the ghost said in a morose tone.

"You're Nathan, right?" he replied.

The ghost cocked his head to the side. "You need to do it and do it quickly."

"I'll take that as a yes, you're Nathan."

"You need to release me from my misery."

"Right." Jacob cleared his throat. "Guess there's not much chance to let off some steam at the local pub when you're trapped in a house like this for all eternity, is there?"

Nathan's expression darkened. "I don't particularly care for your flippant tone, sir."

"Sorry, it's just that I'm not used to having face-to-face time with spirits. Especially ones who seem to know what's going to happen to them."

"It's possible for me to show myself to those who do not have the gift of sight."

"Amanda can see you," Jacob said.

"She can. But she can't help me. In fact, I fear that she may change her mind about exorcising us. And you must make her go through with it."

"She's not going to change her mind. If there's one thing I can guarantee you about Amanda it's that she does her job to the letter."

"You're in love with her." It wasn't a question.

"Is it really that obvious?" Jacob studied the translucent man in front of him for a moment. "I have *definitely* lost my edge. It's embarrassing, really."

"The clock worked its magic on you both, didn't it?"

"It did." Jacob grinned, remembering. "Thanks for the warning, by the way."

The barest glimpse of a smile appeared on Nathan's lips. "Had you not been the one for her there would have been nothing to fear."

"Which means what, exactly?"

"The enchantment only works to bring those together who were already destined for love. All others it passes by."

"That's definitely debatable."

"You've told her of your feelings?"

"At the moment she can read my mind so it's a little hard to hide something like that, even though I might like to."

"So *she* is the one who denies it." Nathan's lips thinned. "No wonder you're still feeling the negative effects of the spell."

Jacob frowned. "You're saying we're feeling the negative effects because she refuses to believe what we have is real?"

"My Catherine denies her heart and the result is our imprisonment in this house." He drew in a long breath he definitely didn't need, being dead. "I can't continue like this. Unable to touch her, only able to see her for such a short time. It's torture. There is only one answer and that is for us to be exorcised from this house. I know your Amanda can grant us that. It may not give us heaven together but it will finally give us peace."

"Damn," Jacob said. "And I thought I was acting way emo this week. You're definitely the winner."

"Emo?" Nathan frowned. "What is emo?"

"Emotional. Angsty. Woe-is-me, etcetera."

Nathan's gaze sparked. "I apologize if I fail to see the humor in this situation."

"Obviously." Jacob shook his head and tried not to smile. Really, it wasn't all that funny. Well, it kind of was.

Nathan was *him*, after all. A darker, bitterer version anyhow. In love with a woman who refused to accept her own feelings at face value. Who would push away a chance at happiness in order to stay true to her rigid beliefs.

They were obviously both screwed.

"Please," Nathan said. "You must make sure that your Amanda follows through with the exorcism. I can't bear to see Catherine again, for seeing her only reminds me that we can never truly be together."

"You really don't think there's any other solution here?"

"The spell that binds us is strong."

"We're planning to destroy the clock hoping that will break the spell."

"You can try," Nathan shook his head. "But the magic is already inside of us. It may do nothing at all but take us deeper into despair."

"*Total* emo," Jacob said under his breath.

There was a crashing sound and a short scream that he recognized as Amanda's. With a last look at the spirit, he turned away and ran down the hall to the drawing room.

Amanda lay on the ground unconscious. His stomach lurched and he ran to her side, falling to his knees next to her. He stroked the dark hair off her forehead. He could see where she'd hit her head, a trickle of blood at her hairline.

But she was breathing and her heart beat regularly which eased his mind a little. He considered carrying her to his car and taking her to a hospital, but just as he began to gather her into his arms her eyelids fluttered before opening up completely.

Her gaze went directly to his but she didn't say anything right away.

"You hit your head," he stated the obvious.

"Ow," she replied.

He brushed his lips over her forehead. "Honestly, I leave you for a few minutes and you go tripping over the furniture."

"I...I'm clumsy like that."

"Obviously."

"Also..." she hesitated. "Catherine pushed me when she found out why we were here."

A surge of anger moved through him. "I'll kill her."

She smiled. "Funny."

"Where is she now?"

"I'm sure she's around. Help me up."

He got to his feet and pulled Amanda up to a standing position.

"You're sure you're okay?" he asked.

"I think so." Amanda swallowed. "I...I had a vision. A major one."

"While you were knocked out or before?"

"During. I thought it was a dream, but it was too vivid. I saw Catherine's wedding day. And the aunt who enchanted the clock in the first place—I saw her, too. I actually got into her head."

He looked amazed by this, but there was no doubt in his expression of what she was telling him. "And?"

"And it wasn't to be cruel. It was to try to help her niece, whom she felt was making the wrong choice by marrying her husband."

"The one who killed her?"

"Yes."

"I'd say she made the wrong choice."

"Yeah." She sucked in a deep breath. "And Nathan was there, too. He was her butler. They wanted each other desperately but they wouldn't give in to their feelings. That's why Rose gave them a little...*push*." Something else came into her mind then, a stray thought from Jacob. "You saw him? Nathan?"

He raised an eyebrow. "I can't say that I'll miss you being able to poke around in my head at your leisure."

"I can't help it when you're this close to me." So close she could feel the heat from his body. It was very distracting.

"Yeah, I see dead people." He grinned. "I've always wanted to say that. Anyhow, he let me see him because he wanted to talk to me. He and I have a lot in common, actually."

"Really? Like what?"

"Like the fact we're both crazy about crazy women."

She chewed her bottom lip. "Definitely sounds like a curse, doesn't it?"

His grin faded at the edges. "Right. Well, he's giving two thumbs up to the exorcism. He's ready for it to be over."

"That makes one of them."

"Catherine isn't keen on getting obliterated?" he asked, wryly. "How odd."

"She kind of freaked, actually. Thus the pushing."

"So she's giving you a hard time. Doesn't mean we hold off. We go through with the exorcism as planned, right?"

She pressed her lips together.

He studied her. "You're not having second thoughts, are you?"

"No, of course not. It's just...they're kind of like us in a way, aren't they?"

"You see that, too?"

She nodded. "Both trapped by magic."

"Trapped," he repeated, and his voice had turned cold again. "Right. Well, I think I've personally had just about enough of that magic. I'm not going to wait until the exorcism is over. I'm going to take care of the clock now."

She was surprised. "Now?"

"What, you wanted to wait? For what? It's not going to change anything."

"No, but—"

He shook his head, his expression sad. "I'm in love with you, Amanda."

He'd said it out loud. It was one thing to hear it in his thoughts...and even then it had been slightly uncertain. This? This was decisive. *He loved her.*

"Jacob—" she began, not knowing exactly how to respond to that.

"I don't think getting rid of that clock is going to make any damn difference to anyone but you. So that's what I'm going to do."

He turned away and stormed out of the room.

She could hear his thoughts echoing in her mind, a little harsher than what he'd said out loud.

I'm going to tear it apart and then burn it. If she wants this over, then it'll be over. I can't take it anymore.

She stood in the drawing room alone for a few moments as the certainty of his decision washed over her.

He was going to destroy the clock. Burn it. Break the spell.

It's what she'd been telling herself she wanted since this began. The only thing tying her to Mystic Ridge and keeping her from a new, normal life was this strange and intense passion she felt for Jacob.

It's not real, the familiar refrain sang in her head.

But the thought didn't keep the panic from welling in her chest. In fact, it became a full-on wave of anxiety.

No. I can't lose this feeling, she thought suddenly. *I can't lose him!*

Still feeling dizzy from hitting her now-aching head, she started for the stairs, taking them two at a time until she got to the top. She rushed along the hallway to the familiar bedroom.

Jacob was in front of the clock, a sharp ax clutched in his right hand. He looked over his shoulder.

"Where'd you get the ax?" she asked tensely.

"I conjured it out of thin air. Or from my trunk where I keep the rest of my arsenal."

"Oh."

"I can take care of this myself," he said. "You don't have to be here."

She exhaled shakily. "Don't do it."

"Excuse me?"

She closed the distance between them and grabbed the weapon out of his hand. "Don't take the clock apart."

He raised both his eyebrows. "Are you possessed?"

"Not the last time I checked, although I guess it's possible."

"Should I go get the holy water just to make sure?"

"Just listen to me for a second, would you?"

"Oh, believe me, I'm all ears."

What is she doing? his thoughts echoed in her ears. *She wanted this and now she's stopping me? The woman is certifiable.*

"You're right, I did want this," she said. "But now I don't. I don't want you to burn the clock."

"If we don't burn it we won't be able to break the spell."

"I know."

His brow furrowed and he studied her intensely, a jumble of thoughts speeding through his head. "What the hell are you talking about?" he growled.

Her head ached. "I know it sounds crazy—"

"It does."

"But...but I don't want to lose this. What we have between us. I've never felt this way before. I guess it scared me. But even if it's only made of magic, I don't want it to go away."

He stared at her for a few moments. "You're serious about this, aren't you?"

She nodded.

"You'd rather stay cursed than risk losing what we have?"

"I know it sounds crazy, but it's true. I didn't know how much this means to me, how much *you* mean to me, until I realized it was going to be taken away."

Kind of like how Catherine had been blasé about her and Nathan's relationship until she faced the prospect of being exorcised and forced apart. That was what had done it for Amanda. Seeing that grief in Catherine's eyes, that sense of impending loss, had made her realize how deep her feelings for Jacob were. She didn't want to lose him, either.

It wasn't just amazing sex. It was so much more than that.

His look was grim. "So that means you'll still be able to read my mind and I can make you tell the truth."

"That's right."

"That's no damn way to live."

"I can deal with it," she said, with more certainty than she'd ever felt before.

His lips thinned. "Well, maybe I can't."

That answer, not previewed in his thoughts, cut into her. "No?"

He shook his head. "You said it yourself. This isn't real, this is all just an illusion." He leveled his gaze with hers. "Until you change your mind about that I don't think we have anything else to discuss here."

This is real, his thoughts told her. *You're just too wrapped up in having your life make perfect sense when life doesn't make sense. It never has and it never will. And that's what's so great about it.*

He closed the distance between them and kissed her hard. She groaned against his lips. It was insane, the way he made her feel. Even the briefest touch was enough to send her over the edge.

He reached down to slide his hands under her skirt. He cupped her panty-free bottom and pull her up against the hard bulge in his pants as their kiss deepened.

She knew she wanted him—there was no denying that he could turn her on as easily as a light switch—but something still bothered her.

Was it that he represented everything that was strange and unusual? Everything that her mother had always told her was wrong? The same things she was mercilessly teased about in school? Not even the teachers had intervened unless things got really bad and even then all they usually did was give her a tissue to wipe her tears.

Jacob embraced his psychic abilities. He didn't find

anything wrong with them. He didn't find anything wrong with *her*.

The fault, obviously, lay with her. She was stubborn and messed-up and neurotic and she gave him a harder time than anyone else probably ever had in his life.

But he still thought he was in love with her.

Why would he love her?

She laughed then, against his lips, as something very important began to make sense to her. She wasn't rejecting him by refusing to believe what she felt was real. She was rejecting herself. Because if she truly believed this was more than magic, she'd have to accept who and what she was once and for all. If she loved Jacob, despite his strangeness, she'd have to love herself, too.

But she'd never loved herself. There was always some fault, even above and beyond her abilities. That had just seemed the best area to focus her self-loathing on.

She pulled away from him and he let her go, his arms dropping slackly to his sides.

"I don't know what else to do here, Amanda," he said. "I give up."

She looked at him, then. Really looked. He stood next to the clock that ticked away the minutes toward midnight— it was currently eleven-thirty. The clock that Rose Embry had enchanted a hundred years ago to help her niece find true love.

And suddenly, as Amanda looked at Jacob Caine, she saw the truth, as well. It made her gasp and tears welled in her eyes.

The very next moment, a bolt of lightning-hot pain went through Amanda's brain and her knees buckled. Jacob caught her, his brows furrowed and drawn together.

"Did you feel that?" Amanda asked weakly.

"I swear, this spell is going to make my head explode."

"Mine, too."

"Pain's gone. Are you okay?"

She nodded. She was okay but the concerned expression Jacob gave her was almost worth more agony. He'd probably felt exactly the same amount of pain as she had, but his first concern was with her well-being.

"What was that?" he asked. "More magic?"

"I think so."

"You can let go of me now," she said.

"Sorry." He released her again. "What can I say? Hard to keep my hands to myself. I do wish right now that you were wearing panties. Or possibly a chastity belt of some kind."

"I will be sending you a bill for new lingerie."

His attention was focused on her lips. "Maybe...maybe I was hasty in my decision. I guess there's no reason for us to chop up the clock tonight. We're not on a deadline, are we?"

"No deadline," she agreed. "Other than my moving three hundred miles away from town tomorrow."

He frowned. "I keep forgetting that little fact."

"That makes one of us."

He gave her a small smile. "So what does this mean? How can we possibly make this mutually acceptable curse work for us? Weekend booty calls? I mean, I'm not ruling those out, but I would like something a little more meaningful. Does that make me less of a macho guy to admit that?"

She smiled. He hadn't figured it out yet, had he?

She closed her eyes and tried to listen in on his thoughts but there was only silence now.

The spell had been broken.

It had been broken the moment she realized the truth—she loved Jacob, and that love was real. The clock's enchantment had helped draw back the layers of protection they'd had over their hearts and egos until they couldn't resist what they both already knew down deep.

She'd never hated him. Not from the very first moment they met.

She'd hated how he'd made her feel with an ill-placed mention of her despised nickname, Amanda the Strange. But he hadn't meant anything cruel by it. She'd stayed away from him as much as she could because the strong feelings she'd had for him from the very beginning—that love at first sight—had never faded. It had scared her so she'd buried it down deep.

Way deep.

No wonder his dating history had upset her. She'd been insanely jealous.

She loved him. This self-proclaimed, card-carrying psychic freak. And he loved her in return.

The clock knew it. The clock hadn't taken a simple no for an answer.

Stupid enchanted clock.

She gave it an amused glare as she silently thanked a witch from a hundred years ago.

They would have remained "cursed" until the day Amanda admitted and accepted that her love for Jacob was the real thing. She honestly didn't know if destroying the clock would have changed a damn thing.

The fact that the spell had been broken with only her thoughts made her realize that Jacob's feelings for her were the real thing, as well.

"Amanda," Jacob said, frowning. "You have the strangest look on your face. Are you absolutely sure you're not possessed?"

She drew him to her and she kissed him again. Just a soft one, a brush of her lips against his. "Almost positive."

"Maybe you have a concussion. You did bang your head really hard earlier. Actually, that would explain how you're acting right now."

"Shh." She kissed him again, and though his body was tense, he didn't resist.

At least, not for a while. Then he stepped back from her, his eyes haunted. "I don't know what you want from me."

She smiled. "I just want you."

"I suppose that could easily be arranged." He glanced at the bed and she followed his line of sight.

"An excellent idea, but I have something I need to take care of first," she said.

"The ghosts?"

She nodded.

"Nathan really wants it to be over. Hell, maybe I'll want it to be over in a hundred years." He gave her a tense smile. "We'll have to wait and see."

She took his hand. "Come on. I need your help. Just follow my lead and play along, okay?"

"Okay." He frowned. He had no idea what she was about to do.

The thought made it even more exciting for her.

16

JACOB COULD use a drink. A big one. Normally he knew what to expect from Amanda. Over the last four days he felt as if he'd gotten to know her very well. She was cold and analytical—kind of like a really hot Vulcan—but at the moment, she was acting so strangely and unpredictably.

She seemed oddly exuberant about the exorcism she was about to perform. It seemed like something one should do with respect or reverence for the spirits who were about to be drop-kicked into the next dimension. He didn't know much about exorcisms, admittedly, but he did know they weren't pleasant—for the exorcist or the exorcized.

Amanda seemed downright...*jubilant*.

He still couldn't believe he'd agreed to leave the curse as it was. It wasn't the best answer, but he'd honor her decision. For now. He was completely and totally convinced that what he felt wasn't the result of a spell. But was he willing to test that theory at the risk of losing Amanda?

Not for a hundred years or so.

Although he would prefer not to become an angsty dead guy if he could help it.

"Catherine," Amanda said sharply as they entered the drawing room. "Please show yourself to both of us."

There was silence.

"Catherine," Amanda said again. "I have the ability to make you appear if I have to. I don't want to have to do that."

Before Jacob's eyes the outline of a woman appeared and it filled in to reveal an attractive blonde in old-fashioned clothes. So this was Catherine, huh? She was very cute. He could see why somebody like Nathan might be persuaded to go on a one-way trip to emo-town for her.

Still, he didn't like that she'd pushed Amanda earlier. The spirit was just damn lucky that she hadn't been more seriously hurt.

Catherine's expression was severe. Severely *pissed.*

"Leave this house," Catherine said evenly.

"I kind of like it here," Amanda replied. Jacob raised an eyebrow at her oddly sassy tone. "I might stay for a bit longer."

"All I ask is that you leave Nathan and me in peace."

"Let me get this straight," Amanda said. "Nathan was your butler."

"That is correct."

"And you had an affair with him when you were married. Because of the spell that your aunt put into the clock, you couldn't keep your hands off his fabulous body."

Catherine's lips thinned. "We were intimately involved."

"Believe me, I know you were. Did I mention the first time I was here I got a vision of you two intimately involved?" She patted the sofa. "Right here?"

Catherine's eyes widened. "We were swept away by passion. It was impossible to resist."

"I know." Amanda glanced over at Jacob then. "Trust me. I know."

He was confused. What the hell was she doing?

"But you weren't really in love with him," Amanda continued.

"Any strong emotions were caused by the enchantment," Catherine said. "Although it's true Nathan believes we transcended that."

"But you don't believe that."

The spirit didn't answer right away. "I don't understand where these questions are leading."

That makes two of us, Jacob pushed his thoughts at Amanda. *This is seriously unnecessary. What are you doing?*

She ignored him. Which was strange since he'd asked her a direct question she should have felt compelled to answer.

"You were very upset when you learned why I'd returned," Amanda said pointedly. "You were beside yourself with grief at the thought of losing Nathan. That doesn't seem the reaction of someone who isn't truly in love."

A trace of fear flickered in Catherine's gaze.

Why are you taunting her? he thought. *Just get this over with so we can leave. You're making me feel sorry for her.*

"My reaction was mostly due to not having seen him in some time since he's been avoiding me," she said. "I would want the chance to say a proper farewell."

"Right." Amanda paused. "Then I'm very sorry to inform you that Nathan has been exorcised. He's gone. The last thing he said was that he loved you and he'd miss you."

Catherine was so still Jacob thought she had turned into a transparent statue.

"He's gone?" She said it so quietly it was barely audible.

"He said that you never loved him so it wouldn't matter. He asked for it. He wanted to go." Amanda turned to Jacob. "Isn't that right?"

He frowned at her so hard it hurt. "Yeah...that's right.

Poor guy. He was ready to leave here so much he was practically begging for us to do it."

Amanda gave him a small smile.

What the hell?

And then it dawned on him what she was doing. His eyes widened.

Do you honestly think this is going to work? he asked her silently.

Again she ignored his direct question. *Weird.*

Catherine continued to stand in place, her arms slack at her sides, her face contorted with grief. Silver streaks moved down her cheeks as she cried silently.

"No," she whispered, shaking her head. "He can't be gone. He can't...I...we were supposed to be together. How will I ever be able to find him again?"

"What difference does it make?" Amanda asked. "You didn't really love him. I'd think this would be a relief for you both. Finally you're free."

Rage finally flashed in Catherine's ghostly eyes and Jacob curled his arm around Amanda's waist to pull her back a few feet. He knew that an angry ghost could do some serious damage if it wanted to. A simple push was only a glimpse of the supernatural power that could be unleashed.

But the fury faded quickly until there was only sadness.

"It's true," Catherine said shakily. "I've denied it for all this time, but it must be true. If it wasn't, I wouldn't feel like this." She looked at Amanda. "My aunt was right, wasn't she? She was right about everything. *I loved him.* I tried to deny it. I tried to push it away, but I couldn't. And now he's gone forever."

"You loved him," Amanda repeated. "Are you sure about that?"

"Yes."

The very next moment, Catherine gasped loudly and a strange ripple of blinding white light spread over her ghostly form before disappearing. She looked at her hands. "What just happened?"

Nathan took form across the room. "What happened is that we're free. Finally."

Catherine stared at Nathan, covering her mouth with her hand in shock. "But...you're gone. I...I don't understand. She said she exorcised you."

He moved closer to her. "She told you what you had to hear to finally make you admit the truth to yourself."

"The truth."

He nodded. "That you love me as much as I love you. I knew you did. All this time, I *knew*." He reached out and stroked her cheek. "See? I can touch you again. The spell is finally broken."

Catherine tentatively touched him, as well. "I can't believe this."

"It's true."

"I'm sorry it took me so long to see that. I was afraid."

His grin widened. "Better late than never."

She smiled back at him. "I love you, Nathan. Forever."

"I love you, too." He bent toward her to give her their first kiss in a hundred years. When they parted, Catherine looked over at Amanda and Jacob, her eyes glowing with happiness.

"Thank you," she said. "Both of you. So much."

Amanda smiled at her and felt a warmth fill her. She was so happy she wouldn't have to perform any exorcisms tonight. "You're very welcome."

The next moment, the two ghosts vanished from the

room in a soft pulse of light. Amanda turned to Jacob, her eyes shiny with tears.

"What in the hell?" he said after a moment. "I feel like I was just forced to watch about eight chick flicks in a row. I seriously need a shower."

She laughed. "That can be arranged."

"Where'd they go?"

"I'm assuming wherever people go when they die. The afterlife."

"They're not trapped here anymore?"

She shook her head. "She broke the spell."

"Damn well took her long enough."

"Some people are pretty thick in the head when it comes to this sort of thing."

Ain't that the truth, he thought. "Here I was expecting to see my first exorcism live and in person."

"We can always rent *The Exorcist.*" She smiled. "But, like I said before, it's a little different in real life. Not nearly as dramatic."

"We can, can we?"

"Definitely."

I don't know, he thought, looking into her eyes. *I'm trying to figure out how this is going to work. You and me. This spell. Are you absolutely sure this is how you want to play it? Are you sure you don't want to destroy the clock now while we're still here?*

She blinked. "What?"

"What do you mean, what? Are you going to answer the question or not?"

"What question?" She looked confused for a moment. "Oh, are you thinking at me again?"

He eyed her warily. "What's going on here?"

"Isn't it obvious?"

"Now you're answering my questions with more questions?"

She looked way too amused. "Ask me something. Anything."

He frowned. "Is the sky blue?"

"Right now it's black. It's almost midnight."

"But is it blue during the day?"

She shook her head. "No, I'm thinking it's more of a magenta. With glitter."

Definitely not the truth, unless in Amanda's world the sky looked like something out of a children's coloring book. "You can't lie to me."

"Sure I can. And just for the record, I can't hear your thoughts anymore. Luckily, what you're thinking is written all over your face."

"It is?" His frown deepened. "Then what am I thinking right now?"

"You're thinking that mind-reading and truth-telling are both part of our curse, and now those things have disappeared. You're thinking that maybe the spell has been broken, but you're not exactly sure how or why."

"That *is* what I'm thinking."

"And now you're starting to think that the only way to break the spell, which as evidenced by what just happened between Catherine and Nathan, is for the more stubborn and annoying partner to admit she's in love with the other."

"That does sound like what's going on in my head right now. Are you sure you can't read my mind anymore?"

"Quite sure. And now you're thinking that the stubborn person can't just say that they love the other out loud, they need to admit it inside themselves as well to know that it's the truth. They can't lie to themselves even though they may have tried really, really hard."

He swallowed. "And what happens then?"

"Then the spell is broken because the enchanted clock's purpose was to make two people realize that they're in love with each other no matter how much they try to deny it to each other or themselves."

"The clock is very strict."

"It is."

"Okay, so I'll admit it, that is what I am thinking right now. The only question is, what are you thinking?"

Amanda placed her hands on Jacob's chest and slid them up over his shoulders. "I'm thinking that I've been kind of stupid."

"No comment."

She smiled at that. "I'm thinking that I've been denying the exact thing that I've wanted more than anything because I didn't think I deserved it."

"And that thing is?"

"You, of course."

Jacob's jaw dropped. "Wait a minute—"

She shook her head and pressed her index finger against his lips. "I tried to convince myself that I wasn't really in love with you, but I was. I *am*. The clock knew it. I guess I've been in love with you since the night I first met you."

He raised one eyebrow, not wanting to believe his own ears. Maybe he'd been knocked unconscious and this was only a dream. "The night at the bar? When I first started at PARA?"

"You called me Amanda the Strange."

"It's a cute nickname."

She grimaced. "Not to me it isn't."

"Oh." He cleared his throat. "Sorry about that, then. Sometimes when I'm nervous I say stupid things."

She laughed. "You're forgiven."

"I can't believe this."

"Believe it." She looked up at him then and a sliver of doubt crept into her expression. "Do you feel any differently now that the spell is broken?"

"Considering I actually had to be told that it was broken, I'm thinking that I don't feel any differently."

"Just checking."

He shook his head. "I still can't believe this."

"Obviously I'm going to have to convince you that I'm in love with you."

"It might take a lot of convincing."

"I have time."

He looked at her very seriously. "What about your big move?"

"Right. That."

"You have a brand-new life waiting for you in New York. If you stay here you'll never feel normal, and isn't that what you want? This mega race to be the most normal woman in North America?"

She shrugged. "I am starting to think that maybe being normal is overrated."

"I could have told you that. In fact, I'm pretty sure I did tell you that a few billion times."

"It's only been four days. Hardly a billion."

"Half a billion." He finally couldn't hold back anymore and he leaned forward to kiss those full, delicious, warm lips of hers. "I love you, Amanda the Strange."

She cringed. "I thought I told you I hate that nickname."

"Sorry." He grinned. "You might have to get used to it.

Because I think it's a seriously sexy pet name for the woman I love."

"Oh, yeah?"

He nodded. "I hate normal chicks. So boring."

"Fine, I forgive you." She grinned and kissed him again.

"I guess we should probably head back to Mystic Ridge."

She shook her head. "Too late. Besides, there is that lovely little bedroom upstairs."

"I like the way you think."

Without another word spoken or thought, he picked her up and carried her quickly up the stairs. He laid her down on the canopied bed where they'd first made love, pulling her dress off over her head and quickly disposing of his own clothes.

He kissed her completely and thoroughly, tasting those lips he'd become addicted to, without any stupid spell as the excuse. He wanted her. He'd wanted her since the first moment he saw her. And now she was his.

"I love you, Jacob," she told him.

He smiled against her lips. "I do love the sound of that."

He timed it so he could slide into her at the stroke of midnight. Seemed appropriate, somehow.

17

SHE WAS awakened by a pounding sound.

Amanda came to the slow realization that her body was entwined with Jacob's body, her arm across his hard chest. He looked so peaceful when he slept. She moved up to kiss him on his lips and his eyelids flickered open.

"'Morning," he said groggily.

"Good morning," she replied.

"So that wasn't just a dream?"

"I'm thinking no." She traced her finger along his whiskered chin. "Is that okay?"

"More than okay." He drew her closer so he could give her a proper kiss.

"What is that sound?"

"Somebody's knocking on the door."

Amanda's eyes widened and she grabbed the bedsheets to pull them up over their blatant display of naked flesh.

The next moment the door to the bedroom swung open and Sheila Davis took a step inside. Her eyes went very big at the sight of the two of them.

"What on earth?" she exclaimed. A big blue vein pulsed on her forehead. "You two? Again? I thought I lodged a complaint with your superiors! I will have you both fired for this continued display of disrespect to my property!"

"Sorry about this," Jacob said, although he couldn't hide an amused expression at Ms. Davis's outrage. "I can't keep my hands off of her. It's like a curse, or something."

"It's sickening."

"Maybe," Jacob said, "if you went out and got some yourself, you wouldn't be so bitchy. No offense intended."

She gasped. "I want you both out of here immediately."

"The ghosts are gone," Amanda said, feeling that she should try to turn this unpleasant moment around a bit.

That doused the flames a little. "Really? That is good news. But it doesn't excuse you for this."

"You're absolutely right," Amanda said. "Very sorry. Really."

"You are?" Jacob asked.

"Well," she shrugged. "Sorry we got caught."

Ms. Davis tapped her foot on the floor. "I'm waiting for you to leave now. Since my supernatural infestation has been taken care of, I can get this place ready for my open house."

"This is a gorgeous house," Amanda said. "Needs a lot of work."

"I don't have the time or money to put into repairs. I've been told that we'll probably sell the property and the house will be torn down."

Amanda shook her head. "That's not going to happen."

"No?"

"No."

"And why not?" Ms. Davis asked, now looking a bit curious to find out the answer from the bedsheet-wearing psychic.

"Because I plan to buy this place," Amanda said matter-of-factly. "I think I can refurbish it. I'll keep it as a home away from home. I love this house."

"Buy it?" Jacob asked. "Are you serious?"

She nodded. "I did tell you I had a little nest egg saved up."

"I didn't know it was enough to buy a house, just enough to live in New York for a while."

"Do you have any idea of the cost of living in Manhattan these days?" Amanda smiled at him. "Trust me, I have enough." She looked at Ms. Davis. "So...obviously this is going to be my house soon."

"Well." Ms. Davis looked flustered. "I am pleased to hear that you're interested."

"So if you could lock the door on your way out?" Amanda instructed. "I'd really appreciate it."

Ms. Davis's gaze swept over the two of them. "I'll have my Realtor contact you immediately."

"Better make it a few hours," Amanda suggested.

Ms. Davis left.

"A few hours?" Jacob asked. "I think you might be overestimating my post-enchantment stamina."

"I'm very willing to test that theory," she said and kissed the man she was completely and totally in love with. There was nothing strange about the way he made her feel.

Her mother would definitely hate him.

She was strangely okay with that.

* * * * *

*Celebrate 60 years of pure reading pleasure
with Harlequin®!
Just in time for the holidays,
Silhouette Special Edition® is proud to present
New York Times bestselling author
Kathleen Eagle's
ONE COWBOY, ONE CHRISTMAS*

Rodeo rider Zach Beaudry was a travelin' man—
until he broke down in middle-of-nowhere South
Dakota during a deep freeze. That's when an angel
came to his rescue....

"**D**on't die on me. Come on, Zel. You know how much I love you, girl. You're all I've got. Don't do this to me here. Not *now*."

But Zelda had quit on him, and Zach Beaudry had no one to blame but himself. He'd taken his sweet time hitting the road, and then miscalculated a shortcut. For all he knew he was a hundred miles from gas. But even if they were sitting next to a pump, the ten dollars he had in his pocket wouldn't get him out of South Dakota, which was not where he wanted to be right now. Not even his beloved pickup truck, Zelda, could get him much of anywhere on fumes. He was sitting out in the cold in the middle of nowhere. And getting colder.

He shifted the pickup into Neutral and pulled hard on the steering wheel, using the downhill slope to get her off the blacktop and into the roadside grass, where she shuddered to a standstill. He stroked the padded dash. "You'll be safe here."

But Zach would not. It was getting dark, and it was already too damn cold for his cowboy ass. Zach's battered body was a barometer, and he was feeling South Dakota, big time. He'd have given his right arm to be climbing into a hotel hot tub instead of a brutal blast of north wind. The right was his free arm anyway. Damn thing had lost altitude, touched some part of the bull and caused him a scoreless ride last time out.

It wasn't scoring him a ride this night, either. A carload of teenagers whizzed by, topping off the insult by laying on the horn as they passed him. It was at least twenty minutes before another vehicle came along. He stepped out and waved both arms this time, damn near getting himself killed. Whatever happened to *do unto others?* In places like this, decent people didn't leave each other stranded in the cold.

His face was feeling stiff, and he figured he'd better start walking before his toes went numb. He struck out for a distant yard light, the only sign of human habitation in sight. He couldn't tell how distant, but he knew he'd be hurting by the time he got there, and he was counting on some kindly old man to be answering the door. No shame among the lame.

It wasn't like Zach was fresh off the operating table— it had been a few months since his last round of repairs— but he hadn't given himself enough time. He'd lopped a couple of weeks off the near end of the doc's estimated recovery time, rigged up a brace, done some heavy-duty taping and climbed onto another bull. Hung in there for five seconds—four seconds past feeling the pop in his hip and three seconds short of the buzzer.

He could still feel the pain shooting down his leg with every step. Only this time he had to pick the damn thing up, swing it forward and drop it down again on his own.

Pride be damned, he just hoped *somebody* would be answering the door at the end of the road. The light in the front window was a good sign.

The four steps to the covered porch might as well have been four hundred, and he was looking to climb them with a lead weight chained to his left leg. His eyes were just as screwed up as his hip. Big black spots danced around with tiny red flashers, and he couldn't tell what was real and what wasn't. He stumbled over some shrubbery, steadied himself on the porch railing and peered between vertical slats.

There in the front window stood a spruce tree with a silver star affixed to the top. Zach was pretty sure the red sparks were all in his head, but the white lights twinkling by the hundreds throughout the huge tree, those were real. He wasn't too sure about the woman hanging the shiny balls. Most of her hair was caught up on her head and fastened in a curly clump, but the light captured by the escaped bits crowned her with a golden halo. Her face was a soft shadow, her body a willowy silhouette beneath a long white gown. If this was where the mind ran off to when cold started shutting down the rest of the body, then Zach's final worldly thought was, *This ain't such a bad way to go.*

If she would just turn to the window, he could die looking into the eyes of a Christmas angel.

* * * * *

Could this woman from Zach's past
get the lonesome cowboy to come in
from the cold...for good?
Look for
ONE COWBOY, ONE CHRISTMAS
by Kathleen Eagle
Available December 2009 from
Silhouette Special Edition®

Silhouette *Desire*

**FROM *NEW YORK TIMES*
BESTSELLING AUTHOR**

DIANA
PALMER

THE
MAVERICK

**A BRAND-NEW
LONG, TALL
TEXAN STORY**

SD76982

REQUEST YOUR FREE BOOKS!

2 FREE NOVELS
PLUS 2
FREE GIFTS!

HARLEQUIN®

Blaze™

Red-hot reads!

HARLEQUIN® HISTORICAL:
Where love is timeless

**From chivalrous knights
to roguish rakes, look for the
variety Harlequin® Historical
has to offer every month.**

COMING NEXT MONTH
Available November 24, 2009

#507 BETTER NAUGHTY THAN NICE Vicki Lewis Thompson, Jill Shalvis, Rhonda Nelson
A Blazing Holiday Collection
Bad boy Damon Claus is determined to mess things up for his jolly big brother, Santa. Who'd ever guess that sibling rivalry would result in mistletoe madness for three unsuspecting couples! And Damon didn't even have to spike the eggnog….

#508 STARSTRUCK Julie Kenner
For Alyssa Chambers, having the perfect Christmas means snaring the perfect man. And she has him all picked out. Too bad it's her best friend, Christopher Hyde, who has her seeing stars.

#509 TEXAS BLAZE Debbi Rawlins
The Wrong Bed
Hot and heavy. That's how Kate Manning and Mitch Colter have always been for each other. But it's not till Kate makes the right move—though technically in the wrong bed—that things start heating up for good!

#510 SANTA, BABY Lisa Renee Jones
Dressed to Thrill, Bk. 4
As a blonde bombshell, Caron Avery thinks she's got enough attitude to bring a man to his knees. But when she seduces hot playboy Baxter Remington, will she be the one begging for more?

#511 CHRISTMAS MALE Cara Summers
Uniformly Hot!
All policewoman Fiona Gallagher wants for Christmas is a little excitement. But once she finds herself working on a case with sexy captain D. C. Campbell, she's suddenly aching for a different kind of thrill….

#512 TWELVE NIGHTS Hope Tarr
Blaze Historicals
Lady Alys is desperately in love with Scottish bad boy Callum Fraser. And keeping him out of her bed until the wedding is nearly killing her. So what's stopping them from indulging? Uhh…Elys's deceased first husband, a man very much alive.

www.eHarlequin.com